✿ 武陵译学丛书

本书受湖南省哲学社会科学基金项目"威廉·卡洛斯·威廉斯早期诗歌中的印象主义研究"（14WLH34）、湖南省教育厅项目"现象学视野下威廉·卡洛斯·威廉斯早期诗歌中的印象主义研究"（16C1324）资助

Impressionism in William Carlos Williams'
Early Poetry 威廉·卡洛斯·威廉斯
早期诗歌中的印象主义

李 慧 著

西南交通大学出版社
·成都·

图书在版编目（ＣＩＰ）数据

威廉·卡洛斯·威廉斯早期诗歌中的印象主义 =
Impressionism in William Carlos Williams' Early
Poetry：英文 / 李慧著. —成都：西南交通大学出版
社，2017.11
　　ISBN 978-7-5643-5903-4

　　Ⅰ.①威… Ⅱ.①李… Ⅲ.①威廉斯（William,
Carlos Williams 1883-1963）–诗歌研究 – 英文 Ⅳ.
①I712.072
　　中国版本图书馆 CIP 数据核字（2017）第 280297 号

Impressionism in William Carlos Williams' Early Poetry
威廉·卡洛斯·威廉斯早期诗歌中的印象主义

李　慧　著

责 任 编 辑	赵玉婷
封 面 设 计	曹天擎
	西南交通大学出版社
出 版 发 行	（四川省成都市二环路北一段 111 号
	西南交通大学创新大厦 21 楼）
发 行 部 电 话	028-87600564　028-87600533
邮 政 编 码	610031
网　　　址	http://www.xnjdcbs.com
印　　　刷	四川煤田地质制图印刷厂
成 品 尺 寸	170 mm × 230 mm
印　　　张	11.25
字　　　数	202 千
版　　　次	2017 年 11 月第 1 版
印　　　次	2017 年 11 月第 1 次
书　　　号	ISBN 978-7-5643-5903-4
定　　　价	68.00 元

Acknowledgements

My gratitude first goes to Prof. Ou Hong, who has always been helpful and patient to me. Under his guidance, I benefit a lot and my knowledge of literature studies is broadened.

I am especially grateful to the members of many kind scholars for their insightful suggestions: Prof. Huang Jiayou, Prof. Li Zhiming, Prof. Pu Ruoqian, Prof. Zhang Guangkui and Prof. Zhang Yuejun. Their close reading of the book improved my work immeasurably. Their suggestions strengthened the arguments in my dissertation.

I am grateful to all the Epsians for their encouragement. Without their constant support, it is impossible for me to accomplish this book.

I would also like to express my thanks to my family for their warm help and support in my study and in the book writing.

PREFACE

The poetry of William Carlos Williams often lives in that imaginative space between visual and verbal art. Some critics have already noted the visual element in his poetry and claimed that Williams' verse is very similar to painting. They examine the relationship between cubism, dadaism and the poetry of Williams. The critics recognize that there is more than a casual relationship between Williams' poetry and the visual arts. These critics have laid a solid foundation for later studies. In order to understand the significance of Williams' poetry, one must consider the visual techniques Williams perfects during his poetic career. Among the major schools of modern painting, impressionism plays a more significant role in the history of the modern arts, greatly owing to its spirit of innovation. As a poet who is enthusiastic about painting from childhood, Williams was unavoidably influenced by the spirit of impressionism in his early time. While, what are its concrete influences on the poetry of Williams? On the basis of the important notions of impressionism the present research intents to explore the similarities between the techniques of impressionism and the early poetry of Williams.

As the fountain of modernist arts, impressionism breaks away from the Academy with a brand new version of the world, focuses on depicting the environment that surrounds them with special attention to light, its transitory and changing qualities on the landscape. As a literary style growing out of impressionism, literary impressionism aims to a depiction in literature of a certain scene, character or emotion. With the style, the author presents the object as it is heard, felt and seen in a single passing moment. Williams' sharp perception in painting enables him to take inspirations from the ideas of impressionism and his poetry demonstrates the conspicuous techniques and stylistic features of impressionism. In his early works, we can find obvious traces of the techniques of impressionism.

On the basis of the important notions of impressionism, the research analyzes impressionism in Williams' early poetry from the following seven chapters. Chapter One is an introduction to the book. The second chapter traces back to the influences on Williams in visual arts. With a close study of the culture of Williams' time, his own experience, and his early poetry, a useful sense of the visual arts background to Williams' early poetry is gained by starting with his earliest poetry and his important early relationships with his mother, who had great artistic talents and once studied art in Paris, his brother Edgar, Ezra Pound, and some painters of his time. Chapter Three explores an important impressionist characteristic, the interplay between the observer and the observed, in the early writing of Williams. Impressionism suggests impressionistic artwork is the interplay between the observer and the observed. Similar to it, the contact between mind and thing (through the agency of the senses) is justly advocated in Williams' poetics. The fusion of the individual's consciousness with the world creates a unity between visual appearance and mental reality. Reality is seen as a harmony of illusion and reality. Williams asserts that readers and the poet should work as co-maker to complete the work; the reader is invited with their imagination to learn complexities underlying the "simplicity" of the materials. Chapter Four works on the characteristics of a most important notion of impressionism, the act of perception, in Williams' early poetry. Williams has said the poem's "sensuality" is the poem's rootedness in the physical world of actuality. The characteristics of impressionist perception, the fresh relationship with the world, the immediacy of impression, the conflict between sensual response and rational response, are so fully responded in Williams' early poems. Chapter Five, entitled "Spatial Time in Williams' Poetry", discusses the impressionistic interpretation of space and time, the harmony of light and color and the philosophy of water in Williams' early poems. Impressionists often emphasize the atmospheric conditions in a certain place at a specific time. Light and its effect on the objects depicted are so important to the impressionist. In literature, the reader is also intended to seize the impressionist works spatially in a moment of time, rather than a time sequence. All these impressionistic techniques are so vividly applied in the early poetry of Williams. Chapter Six focuses on discussing impressionist narrative in Williams' early poetry. Different from the traditional omniscient narrative in which the author's view dominates the way of telling, the impressionist text advocates to render rather than to narrate life. To literary impressionists, limited narrative and fragmental narrative are important new narrative methods to achieve the impressionist effect. The present study intends to articulate how these two impressionist methods are greatly applied in William's early poetry. Chapter Seven is the conclusion of this book.

The innovative spirit of impressionism provides inspirations to Williams in helping him to see the world with a brand new version, know more about human consciousness including more about himself, find his own ways of poem, and establish his particular poetics. The application of the impressionistic techniques in his early poetry enriches the contents and forms of his poems. From then on, Williams in his later years underwent various experiments to incorporate different schools of visual arts into poetry to fashion the themes, and developed techniques in his poetry. His employment of the various visual elements sets an example for the modern poets, shows his strong sense of social responsibility to search for the outlet for the American modernist poetry.

前　言

　　美国现代诗人威廉·卡洛斯·威廉斯的诗歌常常活跃于文字艺术与视觉艺术的想象空间之中。某些评论家已注意到威廉斯诗歌中的视觉元素，并宣称其诗近似于绘画。他们研究威廉斯诗歌与某些现代视觉艺术流派（比如立体主义、达达主义）的联系，认为威廉斯诗歌与视觉艺术之间绝不是一种偶然的关联。从这些视角所进行的研究为后继研究提供了一些背景。若想深入理解威廉斯诗歌所富含的深刻意义与独特魅力，需不断探寻与挖掘诗人在创作生涯中进行的视觉艺术技巧实验，进一步追溯与梳理其诗歌视觉艺术的影响源。作为现代艺术的发源地，印象主义以革新姿态出现于历史舞台，在现代艺术史中占有开先河之重要地位，而威廉斯所生活的时代，正值现代文艺思潮勃兴之时，毋庸置疑，自小酷爱绘画的诗人早年接受过印象主义先锋思想的洗礼。相对于其晚期成熟的艺术创作而言，其早期诗歌（1909 年至 1939 年间）的创作颇为重要，这段时期的作品介于不成熟与成熟之间，这期间诗人的思考相当活跃，承前启后。因此，深入系统研究印象主义对威廉斯早期诗歌的影响就尤其重要。那么，印象主义对威廉斯诗歌的具体影响究竟体现在哪些方面？本书试图以印象主义重要理论观点为线索，运用诗画结合的方法，分析威廉斯早期诗中显现的印象主义元素，发掘其诗歌风格和表现手法与印象主义之间的关联性。

　　19 世纪下叶兴起的印象主义向日益僵化的学院派和传统艺术观念发动大胆的挑战与变革，它以全新的视角审视世界，重视光以及光投射于被描绘的物体上所产生的效果，注重捕捉感觉的瞬间印象。受绘画印象主义技巧和美学观念的启发，20世纪初出现了文学印象主义，它所采用的技巧和达到的效果和印象主义绘画相似，由于文学创作的特质，文学中的印象主义更注意这些瞬间感觉如何转化为情感状态。威廉斯在绘画上的敏锐感悟力使其从印象主义思想中获得诗学灵感，赋予其诗歌强烈的印象主义风格，特别是其早期诗作，显现出明显的印象主义特色。

　　本书共分为七章。第一章为绪论。第二章从威廉斯的诗歌、传记以及书信入手，探溯诗人与现代视觉艺术（特别是印象主义）的缘起。自幼受到擅长绘画的母亲影响，威廉斯与兄弟埃德加对绘画的兴趣由来已久，兄弟间保持着长期的联系与交流。同时，与重要诗人庞德以及同时代的画家朋友德穆斯等人的长期交往与切磋，也是催生威廉斯诗画灵感的重要影响源。第三章阐述印象主义的重要观点"观者与被观者的互动"在威廉斯诗学及其早期诗歌中的体现。威廉斯与印象主义可谓不谋而合，主张个体意识与外部世界的亲密接触，从而在视觉世界与心理世界之间建立起一个合力，实现想象与现实的和谐，他的诗作强烈呼唤读者与作品的互动，吸引读者运用自己的想象去理解材料的"简单性"之中涵盖的"复杂性"。威廉斯"概念只存在于事物之中"的诗学主张与印象主义"观者与被观者的互动"的观点有着强烈共鸣。第四章论述印象主义的另一重要概念"感知行为"在威廉斯早期诗歌中的体现。印象主义坚持从感知出发，主、客体从二元对立走向二元共生，这种打破主客分野的姿态同样符合威廉斯的诗学主张。威廉斯曾说过，诗的"感知性"是诗歌扎根于现实物质世界的根基。本章拟呈现"感知行为"的内涵特征（意识与世界的全新关系、感觉印象的瞬息性、感觉反应与理性反应的冲突）在威廉斯早期诗歌中的突出体现，证明威廉斯明确认同印象主义坚持从感知出发的观点，意识必须是事物之中的意识，思想与事物水乳交融。第五章阐述威廉斯早期诗歌中蕴含的印象主义时空内涵。在这方面，威廉斯早期诗歌的运诗技巧与印象主义技巧明显近似，强调在某一特定时间的某一特定地点里的氛围条件下捕捉事物或情感的瞬息存在，光与色彩的和谐在威廉斯的诗中有着出神入化的运用。"水"作为最能体现光与色的完美结合的意象，一直是印象主义画家和作家们笔下的最爱，印象主义关于水与时间的哲思在威廉斯的水意象诗里更有着淋漓尽致的发挥。第六章阐述印象主义叙事技巧在威廉斯早期诗歌中的运用。威廉斯反对传统的叙事技巧，追求诗歌叙事上的革新与创作自由，印象主义的重要叙事技巧（如：有限叙述、碎片化叙述）在他诗里均有明显体现。通过对传统全知全能叙事的反拨，有限叙述和碎片化叙述的运用揭示现实其实不可能被任何个体所完全理解，诗人在文本中对权威声音的去除，宣示对真理本质的种种假设统统都无效，赋予了读者一种全新的"看"的态度。第七章为结语。

印象主义革新思想给予威廉斯一种"看"的态度，使他对世界、人类意识及其作为人类文明重要成果的诗歌开始全新审视。在其探索新诗新路的早期阶段，印象主义诗学为威廉斯建构自己独具特色的诗学观奠定了理论基础，印象主义视觉艺术元素丰富了威廉斯诗歌的表达内容和表现形式。自此以后，威廉斯毕生不断尝试诗歌实验，继续将继印象主义革新之后如雨后春笋般萌生的其他现代视觉艺术流派（如：立体主义、达达主义等）纷纷融入于诗，在风格和技巧上日臻完善。他对于视觉艺术元素的独特阐释，既确立了他在现代诗坛的重要地位，也为 20 世纪美国新诗开辟了出路。

本书从想象性和感知性诗学观、时空观和叙述方式四个方面详细而周密地论证威廉斯诗歌与印象主义绘画艺术通感的有效性，揭示威廉斯诗歌的先锋性和艺术特征，从而有助于深化国内外威廉斯的诗歌研究。目前，国内外有关威廉斯与视觉艺术的影响关系研究仅提及印象主义对威廉斯诗歌产生过影响，但具体在哪些方面对威廉斯产生了影响，尚未有深入系统研究。本书以印象主义理论为线索，运用诗画结合的方法，专门深入系统研究印象主义对威廉斯早期诗歌的具体影响。这一研究视角和研究方法都属于国内具有开拓性的研究尝试。

由于自身的学术水平有限，书中肯定存在不少欠缺的地方和错误，恳请读者和专家不吝赐教。

Abbreviations

ARI	*A Recognizable Image: William Carlos Williams on Art and Artists*. ed. with an introduction by Bram Dijkstra. New York: New Directions Publishing Corporation, 1978.
Au	*The Autobiography of William Carlos Williams*. New York: New Directions Publishing Corporation, 1967.
CP I	*The Collected Poems of William Carlos Williams*. Volume 1. New York: New Directions Publishing Corporation, 1984.
CP II	*The Collected Poems of William Carlos Williams*. Volume 2. New York: New Directions Publishing Corporation, 1984.
PB	*Pictures from Brueghel*. New York, New Directions Publishing Corporation, 1962.
SE	*The Selected Essays of William Carlos Williams*. New York: New Directions Publishing Corporation, 1969.
SL	*The Selected Letters of William Carlos Williams*. New York: McDowell, Obolensky Inc., 1957.
SLP&W	*The Selected Letters of Ezra Pound and William Carlos Williams*. New York: New Directions Publishing Corporation, 1996.

目录
CONTENTS

Chapter 1

Introduction

1.1 The Motivation of the Project

Born in Rutherford, New Jersey, William Carlos Williams (1883-1963) is known as one of the most outstanding modern American poets. In comparison to artists of his own time who sought a new environment for creativity as expatriates in Europe, Williams lived a remarkably conventional life. A doctor for more than forty years serving the rural town of Rutherford, New Jersey, he relied on his patients, the America around him, and his own ebullient imagination to create a distinctively American verse. He advocated American poetry must be rooted in America as its fount of inspiration and its source of information and subject matter. In his *Autobiography*, he says that a poet must base his ideas and thought on the ordinary lives of people. He drew his subject matter from ordinary surroundings, such as paintings, the change of seasons, flowers, a red wheel barrow, etc. Named as "father of postmodernism American poetry" (Riddel 17), Williams had his own distinct views concerning the nature of poetry, the function of the poet, and the poetic process. The viewpoint of Williams is embodied in his famous doctrine "No ideas but in things" (Ostrom 12).

He devoted all his life to persistent exploration and innovation of poetic form. In his time, modernist poets, including Ezra Pound, were drawn to the strategies of the painters by the nature of the modernist poetic. The years 1909 through 1930s were marked in New York, Paris and London by an unparalleled collaboration between the poets and the painters. Poets painted and the painters wrote. Poets cited painters in their manifestoes, and painters wrote out their painterly theories and incorporated linguistic elements into the visual strategies of their paintings. Perhaps more than any other poet, Williams looked to painting for new strategies to bring to his work. The development of his early poetry is the development of an increasingly complex series of patterns – within poems, and within sequences of his poems – leading up to his 1923 *Spring and All*. Williams' poetry is possessed of the visual characteristics, as many of his poems are apt to create visual pictures in the readers' mind. Like the works of several other poets in the twentieth century, Williams' poetry reflects the influence of many types of visual arts. In this research, the author finds similarities between the early poetry of Williams and the techniques of impressionism. Those paintings which are impressionistic often emphasize the atmospheric conditions in a certain place at a specific time. Light and its effect on the objects depicted are also very important to the impressionist. This impressionistic attitude toward visual art can be applied to poetry as well. Through a close and concentrated observation of Williams' entire body of poetry, the social historical and cultural background of his time and a careful study of the techniques of impressionism and literary impressionism, based on previous studies on Williams' poetics and poetry, the author of the book intends to focus on exploring the impressionist strategies in Williams' early poetry (1909-1939), through social-historical analysis and with close textual attention. Essentially there have been two periods in Williams career, an early period from about the time of 1900 to the 1939, works of which period are collected in *The Collected Poems of William Carlos Williams (1909-1939)*, and a later period is after the publication of

Paterson Ⅳ, during which time he seems to have settled pretty much on one scheme (Ostrom 77). Of the two periods, the earlier is more interesting and important to examine. It is a period of apprenticeship in which – apparently at Pound's insistence – he turned from the conventional poetic modes of the earliest 1900s to newer forms, especially from about the time of *Al Que Quiere!* (1917) to the middle 1940s in which Williams explored and developed various techniques of his own. It is essentially a time when Williams was getting to know himself and the new ways of the poem, and his work from that period is now of little interest other than the historical. With great interest and curiosity, the research aims to reveal the influence of impressionism on his early poetry. In this book, the author plans to interpret more than 30 Williams' early short poems, from the year 1909 to 1939. Impressionism in Williams' poetry is the reflection of the revolution and innovation of his poetry and poetics, and the reflection of his time.

1.2   Literature Review

As a full-time physician, William Carlos Williams made most use of his spare time to write stories, novels, plays, essays as well as poetry. However, until the last few years of his life Williams was almost entirely neglected by the literary critics. Not only the academic critics, but the "little magazine" critics, too, acted, for the most part, as if he did not exist. Some few made passing references to him, and even fewer took him seriously, none wrote of him as a major figure of their time, though, Pound and occasional reviewers in *Poetry* magazine spoke well of Williams. In 1936 Babette Deutsch in his *The Modern Poetry* helped establish an important place for him. Then, as the sections of William's *Paterson* began to come out (the first four of the five sections to be completed appeared between 1940 and 1951), recognition slowly followed; New Directions, publisher of that long poem, brought out the first book on Williams in 1951(by Vivienne Koth). Williams' importance as an influence in modern poetry grew until he became, in the late fifties, perhaps the greatest single force in American poetry. In his later life (he died in his eightieth year in 1963, five years after the last fully finished part of *Paterson*), Williams received various literary prizes and several honorary degrees. And a good more was written about him. Over the last few years Williams has become popular, not only in the avant-garde circles, but also in the academic world, in college courses in American literature. The interest has continued. In 1966, Williams was the first author to be featured on a National Educational Television series broadcast from a hundred stations. Some important characteristics of Williams' poetry result in his leading position in poets of his time.

Concreteness and short line, colloquial tone and idiom characterize Williams' poetry, while probably the most important element is his experiment on the form of poetry. The old methods, he saw, were useless; they were measurements of a language his world did not speak, of an old-world English rather than of a new-world American. As a result, there appears a lot of criticism on Williams and his works. For example, Harry T. Moore's *The Poetic World of William Carlos Williams* (1965) brings together Williams' various sorts of poems, providing a thorough evaluation of Williams' poetry. Mike Weaver's *William Carlos Williams: The American Background* (1971) looks at various sources for Williams' art. *The Early Poetry of William Carlos Williams* (1972, by Rod Townley), after showing how Williams' earliest works reflect conflicting allegiance, both spiritual and literary, follows the poet through the transition years 1910-1917, when he found his own unmistakable poetic voice. In the book, Townley devotes a chapter each to *Kora in Hell: Improvisations* (1920),

Sour Grapes (1921), and *Spring and All* (1923). In the afterword, Townley summarizes his view of the early Williams and looks toward Williams' later life and work. Carl Rapp describes Williams' relation to Romanticism in *William Carlos Williams and Romanticism* (1974), and shows that Williams is very much a part of the Romantic tradition, even though many of his poems seem quite un-Romantic. Dickran Tashjian's *William Carlos Williams and the American Scene 1920-1940* (1979) points out that Williams' cultural significance derives precisely from his marginality during those two decades between the wars – a marginality that deeply shaped his ambiguous and ambivalent perception of the issues of his time. As a quintessential avant-gardist, precisely because Williams grasped the ambiguities of art in America, he guides his readers through the complexities of the American scene during the 1920s and 1930s. The argument of Henry M. Sayre's study in *The Visual Text of William Carlos Williams* (1983) goes against the "traditional" Williams. Its claim is that his last poems, the ones in which his new measure is finally achieved, are meant to be read, with the eye, on the page. The visual dimension of Williams prosody has, furthermore, far-reaching epistemological implications. Stephen Tapscott's *American Beauty: William Carlos Williams and the Modernist Whitman* (1984) investigates Whitman's influence on Williams. To get the immediate evidence of Whitman's "influence" on Williams' poems, Stephen Tapscott puts Williams into the historical context that provoked his response to the Whitmanian "tradition." In *The Early Politics and Poetics of William Carlos Williams* (1987), David Frail's study is best read as a biography of William Carlos Williams' early politics, their relation to his poetics, and their expression in his poems. Bryce Conrad's *Refiguring America* (1990) demonstrates a study of William Carlos Williams' *In the American Grain*. In *William*

Carlos Williams and Transcendentalism: Fitting the Crab in a Box (1992), Ron Callan looks at the work of Ralph Waldo Emerson and Henry David Thoreau as part of the development towards Williams. A good collection of recent criticism about Williams is *Critical Essays on William Carlos Williams* (1995) edited by Stephen Gould Axelrod and Helen Deese. Now some critics have shown an increasing interest in the relationship of literature and medicine in Williams' writing: *Modernism, Medicine, and William Carlos Williams* (1993) by T. Hugh Crawford, and *William Carlos Williams and the Diagnostics of Culture* (1993) by Brain Bremen.

Moreover, some critics have noticed the visual elements in William's works. In *The Hieroglyphics of a New Speech: Cubism Stieglitz, and The Early Poetry of William Carlos Williams* (1969), Bram Dijkstra examines the relationship between cubism[①] and the early poetry of Williams, demonstrates that Williams attempted to emulate the Stieglitz group in focusing on the object itself, delineating it as precisely as possible. In *The Visual Imagination of William Carlos Williams* (1976), Margaret Morgan Starr demonstrates a study of *Pictures from Brueghel*, examines the graphic design of punctuation, line length, and syntax in Williams' poetry. The argument of Marling William supplies a lot of solid biographical influences between Williams and the New York avant-garde in his *William Carlos Williams and the painters*, 1909-1923(1982). In *William Carlos Williams' early poetry: the Visual Arts Background* (1983), Christopher J. MacGowan documents Williams' contact with painters and theories within the modernist visual arts, and applies this background material to a careful study of the poems. Peter Schmidt discusses the relationship between

---

① Cubism is an early-20th-century avant-garde movement pioneered by Pablo Picasso and Georges Braque, joined by Jean Meizinger, JuanGris, et al. that revolutionized European painting and sculpture, and inspired movements in music, literature and architecture.

cubism and the poetry of Williams, and the relationship between dadaism[1] and the poems of Williams in his book *William Carlos Williams, the Arts, and Literary Tradition* (1988). Peter Halter makes a further exploration of the connection between the visual arts and Williams' concept of the modernist poetry in his *The Revolution in the visual Arts and the Poetry of William Carlos Williams* (1994). The perspective analyses of these critics have provided the background for its later study.

The domestic research of Williams' poems did not seriously begin until 1990s. Some articles were published in both minor and major journals, mostly focusing on his language of clarity and conciseness, and on simple and vivid images in his poems. The visual elements in his poetry began to be noted in recent years. The monograph *In the American Grain: On the Pragmatic Poetics of William Carlos Williams* (2006) by Zhang Yuejun is pathbreaking: it demonstrates a study of Williams in the light of American pragmatism, especially that formulated by John Dewey, and shows that Williams' writing is pragmatic and that his pragmatic poetics is deeply engrained in the native tradition of America. Liu Xiaojie in "On the Color Language of William Carlos Williams' Poetry" (2003) and "On the Spatial Consciousness in William Carlos Williams' Poetry" (2009) demonstrates that Williams' poetry is a fusion of painting and poetry.

Moreover, there are also some studies on Williams' acceptance of classical Chinese poetry. Chinese American Scholar Qian Zhaoming's *Orientalism and Modernism: The Chinese Heritage of Pound and Williams* (1995) convincingly demonstrates Po Chu-I as Williams' Chinese craft, tutor and bosom friend. Stephen Field has made a good research of this kind in "'The Cassia Tree': A Chinese Macropoem."(1992) Zhang Yuejun

---

[1] Dada or Dadaism was an art movement of the European avant-garde in the early 20th century. The movement primarily involved visual arts, literature, poetry, art manifestoes, art theory, theatre, and graphic design, and concentrated its anti-war politics through a rejection of the prevailing standards in art through anti-art cultural works.

also discusses the underlying dialogue between Williams and classical Chinese poetry in his monograph.

Compared with the abundant researches on Williams abroad, in China, more introductions to Williams' poetry and poetics should be made in college courses in American literature, more analysis and interpretation of his poetry should be made, and more efforts should be made to the criticism of Williams' marvelous poetry.

1.3 Brief Introduction of Impressionism and Literary Impressionism

Since the research is to study Williams' early poetry from the impressionistic perspective, a brief introduction of impressionism and literary impressionism is necessary.

Impressionism is the name given to the school of painting that started in France in the second half of the 19th century. As a technical term, it made its debut in 1874, used by a journalist whose intention in using it was to make derogatory comments on Claude Monet's painting *Impression, Sunset* (1873, Figure 1), a painting styles impressionism that finds no echo in the then popular aesthetic values. Impressionism defies easy definition. Although it now refers to the most popular movement in Western art, it originated as a term of abuse – applied to an exhibition of works that appeared shockingly sketchy and unfinished. The artists who created these works were united in their rejection of the old, "tame" art encouraged by the official Salon, but their artistic aims and styles varied. They were not only of diverse characters and gifts, but also, to a certain extent, of differing conceptions and tendencies. They did have two fundamental concerns: depicting modern life and painting in the open air. Alfred Sisley, for example, had little interest in anything but landscapes, while Edgar

Chapter 1

Introduction

Degas ardently opposed painting outdoors. Despite their differences, Claude Monet, Berthe Morisot, Auguste Renoir, Camille Pissaro, Alfred Sisley, Gustave Caillebotte, Edgar Degas, Charles Demuth and Mary Cassatt developed a new way of depicting the world around them, and, together with other artists they displayed their work in the "Impressionist exhibitions" held between 1874 and 1886 in modern Paris, which was the catalyst, birthplace, and subject matter of much of Impressionist art. The impressionists of Paris were not alone in their approach to art. Around the world, artists also began to choose modern-day subjects, painted outdoors, used bright colors, and sometimes even called themselves "Impressionists". The works of the impressionists seemed at first glance much revolutionary. This was in itself a break with established customs. It took years of bitter struggle for the impressionists to convince the public to accept their talent. The term, afterward, was also employed to refer to their works, especially of the later 1860s to mid-1880s.

"The most important characteristic of impressionism lies in its insistence on the perceptual reality instead of the conceptual one" (Kronegger 67). That is to say the impressionist painter draws what he actual sees from nature without caring what his mind thinks. The painter is more fond of faithful record of the sensual effect of the object in the sensitive mind, than the representation of the object itself. He gives precedence to his subjective attitude. In order to record the primary impression accurately and precisely, he paints "emphasizing spontaneity and immediacy of vision and reaction" (Smith 3). Nowadays, the term "impressionism" is put into use in a broad sense. Any artist or work that evokes the audience's impressions in a subjective way can be called an impressionist.

Impressionist movement is a good example of the modern spirit. Literary impressionism grew out of impressionism in painting. The term "literary impressionism" was first used by the late nineteenth-century critics to mainly describe the spontaneous, sketchy and unfinished qualities of writing. Alphones Daudet, Jules and Edmond Goncourt, Emile Zola and George Moore associated with and wrote about many of the painters. Henry James, Marcel Proust, Virginia Woolf, Joseph Conrad, Ford Madox Ford and others were acquainted with many of their works.

Impressionist writers have created a new vision of the world. With them, faith in an absolute has disappeared, the world has been relativized. The Cartesian tendency to divide up the world, to fix and determine it, to comprehend and classify, to recognize in the world things we already know, this conceptualization of the world is for the impressionist writer and artist a "thing-in-itself," a reality with no possibility of growth, a dead world (Bender 37).

> Impressionist writers begin with an empirical reality rather than an abstract idea. Reality, for the impressionists, has become a vision of space, conceived as sensations of light and color. Space is no longer a geometrical medium, but a medium of light which the impressionist artist can render by color. Color also does not render depth, but atmosphere. Impressionist writers oppose irregularity and variety of sensations to the order of reason, being convinced that both in nature and in art all beauty is irregular. (Konnegger 30)

What all impressionist writers wish to achieve is harmony, a rhythmical effect of beauty, stressing the autonomy of their creation. Their work reflects dominion of the passing mood over the permanent qualities of life. The sum total of these qualities of impressionist works seems to point to the same underlying forces which are evident in the ideas of the age:

change, flux and instability, detachment.

The most important characteristics of literary impressionism can be found in the following three aspects: it is the interplay between the observer and the observed; impression bridges the two and as the basis of the text, it includes two responses: sensual and rational. The chief goal of literary impressionism is to represent the conflict between the two opposite responses; the narration in the literary impression is limited.

1.4 The Organization of This Book

William Carlos Williams has been researched abroad for more than sixty years. The domestic research of Williams' poems did not begin until 1990s. More efforts should be made to the criticism of Williams' in future research. With a close and concentrated observation of William's early poetry and social-historical background of the twentieth century, based on previous studies on Williams' poetics, the research focuses on demonstrating the impressionism strategies in Williams' early poetry (1909-1939), with impressionist perspective, social-historical analysis and close textual attention. The purpose of this study, then, is to demonstrate the multiform characteristics of impressionism in Williams' early poetry, and describe the affinities between the impressionist painting and his poetry. The present study is an analysis of the similarities between the early poetry of Williams and the techniques of impressionism. In the previous studies on the issue, Williams' use of the techniques is associated with different schools of painting, including precisionism, cubism, and dadaism. As a fountain of modernist arts, impressionism has greatly influenced the development of all schools of modernist painting and the works of some poets in the twentieth century. Yet, its influence on Williams is only mentioned by a few scholars and has scarcely been thoroughly explored.

In terms of the organization of this book, the first chapter is an introduction to the book. The second chapter traces back to the influences on Williams in visual arts. With a close study of the culture of Williams' time, his own experience, and his early poetry, a useful sense of the visual arts background to Williams' early poetry is gained by starting with his earliest poetry and his important early relationships with his mother, who had great artistic talents and once studied art in Paris, his brother Edgar, Ezra Pound, and some painters of his time.

The third chapter explores an important impressionist characteristic, the interplay between the observer and the observed, in the poetic world of Williams. Impressionism suggests impressionistic artwork is the interplay between the observer and the observed. Similar to it, the contact between mind and thing (through the agency of the senses) is justly advocated in Williams' poetics. The fusion of the individual's consciousness with the world creates a unity between visual appearance and mental reality. Reality is seen as a harmony of illusion and reality. Williams asserts that readers and the poems should work as co-maker to complete his work; he invites the readers to use their imagination to learn complexities underlying the "simplicity" of the materials. Williams' famous credo, "no ideas but in things", can be called an echo of the notion of impressionism, the interplay between the observer and the observed.

Chapter Four focuses on analyzing the characteristics of a most important notion of impressionism, the act of perception, in Williams' early poetry. Williams has said the poem's "sensuality" is the poem's rootedness in the physical world of actuality. The characteristics of impressionist perception, the fresh relationship with the world, the immediacy of impression, the conflict between sensual response and rational response, are so fully responded in Williams' early poems. It proves that Williams positively agrees with the outlook of impressionists that an object is not important only in its relationship to the consciousness in which it has appeared, and consciousness must be consciousness of something.

Chapter Five, entitled as "Spatial Time in Williams' Poetry", focuses on discussing the impressionistic interpretation of space and time, the harmony of light and color and the philosophy of water in Williams' early poems. Impressionists often emphasize the atmospheric conditions in a certain place at a specific time. Light and its effect on the objects depicted are so important to the impressionist. In literature, the reader is also intended to seize the impressionist works spatially in a moment of time, rather than a time sequence. All these impressionistic techniques are so vividly applied in the early poetry of Williams.

Chapter Six focuses on discussing impressionist narrative in Williams' early poetry. Different from the traditional omniscient narrative in which the author's view dominates the way of telling, the impressionist text advocates to render rather than to narrate life. To literary impressionists, limited narrative and fragmental narrative are important new narrative methods to achieve the impressionist effect. The present study intends to articulate how these two impressionist methods are greatly applied in William's early poetry. Chapter seven is the conclusion of the book.

Demonstrating these impressionistic features in Williams' early poetry and exploring the sources of his visual art background this book can more fully explain the complexity of Williams' poetics, understand the significance of Williams' verse, and help Williams' readers understand his poetry more deeply.

Chapter 2

Influences of Visual Arts on Williams

Williams' work is often the product of the painters' eyes and the painters' methods. With a close study of the culture of Williams' time, his own experience, and his early poetry, a useful sense of the visual arts background to Williams' early poetry is gained by starting with his earliest poetry and his important early relationships with his mother, who had great artistic talents and once studied art in Paris, his brother Edgar, Ezra Pound, and some painters of his time.

2.1   Williams' Contact with the Visual Arts

The central importance of the visual in Williams' poetry is strikingly emphasized in a short article he wrote for *The Columbia Review* in 1937. He wrote, "Think of the poem as an object, an apple that is red and good to eat – or a plum that is blue and sour – or better yet, a machine for making bolts."[1] In 1929, to the question "What is your strongest characteristic?" posed by the editors of *The Little Review,* Williams replied: "My sight. I like most my ability to be drunk with a sudden realization of value in things others never notice."[2] With Williams' emphasis on sight came, not surprisingly, an abiding, life-long interest in the visual arts.

---

[1] "Poetry." The Columbia Review, ⅩⅨ, Ⅰ (November 1937), 3.
[2] *The Little Review* (May 1929), 87.

Chapter 2
Influences of Visual Arts on Williams

On February 17, 1913, the Armory Show opened in New York. In this huge exhibition, the revolutionary European movements in the visual arts, such as Impressionism, Fauvism, Cubism, and Futurism, were introduced to the general American public for the first time, side by side with a comprehensive show of progressive American art. The exhibition was an object of derision and amusement to the vast majority of visitors and critics alike, but it deeply impressed a number of artists and critics, who were increasingly dissatisfied with the triteness and utter conventionality of the established artistic forms. Their main reaction was one of fascination and excitement: The revolutionary European art threw the provincial and conventional character of most of their own products into sharp relief and created in turn an intense hope for an American art of equal temerity – for an art that would neither ignore what had happened outside America nor withdraw from the crass contemporary world of materialism and science into the creation of spurious idylls based on an anemic idealism. Williams' own comments on the Armory Show reveal his feeling of hope for an imminent fundamental change:

> There was at that time a great surge of interest in the arts generally before the First World War. New York was seething with it. Painting took the lead. We were tinder for Cézanne. I had long been deep in love with the painted canvas through Charles Demuth but that was just the beginning…Then the Armory Show burst upon us, the whole Parisian galaxy, Cézanne at the head, and we were exalted by it. (*Au* 57)

Beside the show, actually in several ways Williams was deeply influenced by visual arts. Introduced into the world of art through his mother's still lives, he had shown a keen interest in painting from the beginning. His early friendship with Demuth, whom he met in 1905 in Philadelphia, was the first of several intimate relationships with painters.

Williams' mother painted, and had studied art in Paris. Her interest in art influenced Williams deeply in his early life. Williams later claimed:

> I was conscious of my mother's influence all though this time of writing...I've always held her as a mythical figure, remote from me, detached, looking down on an area in which I happened to live, a fantastic world where she was moving as a mere or less pathetic figure. Remote, not only because of her Puerto Rican background, but also because of her bewilderment at life in a small town in New Jersey after her years in Paris where she had been an art student. Her interest in art became my interest in art. I was personifying her, her detachment from the world of Rutherford. She seemed a heroic figure, a poetic ideal. I didn't especially admire her; I was attached to her... (Heal 16)

And this interest is expressed in his earliest letters. Writing from the University of Pennsylvania in 1904, he told his mother of a visit to a local painter, a Mr. Wilson, who "was painting in his studio so he gave me an easel, some brushes and I painted a still life." (*SL* 27) In his autobiography Williams identified this early teacher as: "John Wilson...a man in his early fifties, I imagine...a failure of an artist who used to paint, right out of his head, landscapes and cows, pictures 24 × 36 inches or so, that sold as 'art' for from ten to twenty dollars. (*Au* 61)" At the time of the publication of his first book of poems in 1909, he would journey "into the fields along the river...to do some painting as Mr. Wilson had taught me. (*Au* 106)

Little work survives as evidence of this early activity. In the 1950s, when Yale librarian Norman Holmes Pearson questioned Williams on his early painting efforts and suggested including a canvas or two in the Yale collection, Williams depreciated their importance. Although he "painted a little at one time" he told Pearson, "the results are not enlightening, not worth owning." He offered Pearson the landscape oil *The Passaic River* (warning that the painting was "no good") and also what he called "a bold self-portrait" that has some "light in it."[1] (The landscape c.1912 is now at Yale; the portrait c.1914 is at the University of Pennsylvania.) Apart from these two canvases, there remain a few scattered line drawings among Williams' papers at Yale and Buffalo, and some drawings in his 1906 medical class yearbook. This yearbook, for which Williams served as "art editor," contains four line drawings signed "W. C. Williams."

Mrs. Williams' interest in art was also transmitted to Williams' young brother Edgar, who was painting and drawing in college. In early letters to Edgar, Williams often asked for news of his work. In 1904, he wrote, "Tell me what you do in the art line every time you write to me for I am very much interested." Four years later he was still adding "Tell me about your drawings" (*SL* 27). Williams' son, William Eric, has described many paintings on the walls of the Williamses' house at 9 Ridge Road, Rutherford, New Jersey, and noted that among the Hartleys, Demuths and Sheelers "the majority…are water colors done by Dad's brother Edgar."[2]

Williams and his brother, Edgar had tried their hands at painting in their youth – although Williams soon gave it up, probably because his work toward a medical degree required most of his attention. In deciding to focus on poetry, Williams by no means chose to abandon practicing a visual art. He believed that poetry pursued the same goals as painting in the world of images. Even after he had begun to write, he toyed with the idea of becoming a painter for several years. By 1908 Williams was working as

---

[1] Williams, unpublished letter to Norman Holmes Pearson. 20 Sept. 1957, Yale Za 221.
[2] Williams, William Eric. "The House." WCWN 5, No. I (Spring 1979): 3.

an intern in New York. He told Edgar of his rigorous scheme of self-education, which included studying the plants and trees in Bronx Park, visiting the Museum of Natural History, and attending a lecture course on great masters of music. He also explored the Metropolitan Museum, reporting that "with a catalogue I'll soon be able to distinguish a few of the leading characteristics of the principal schools of painting." This eclectic activity was part of his determination, he told Edgar, to "show the world something more beautiful than it has ever seen before." It was all carefully copied down: "I am keeping notes on architecture, landscape and decoration as well as mechanical features which I like in connection with my idea."[1]

Williams quoted Milton to Edgar approvingly: "to feel is living and all poetry must be sensuous." Through its affective power – powers shared by architecture and the other arts – poetry achieves its moral ends: "This is the province of art, to influence the best and as we learn the better and better to influence each other with beauty so shall we perhaps grow to help others and perhaps who can tell in the end we may help many."[2]

Early in 1909 Williams published his first volume of poetry, *Poems*. That summer he journeyed to Leipzig to pursue his medical studies. Viewing "the German art" in terms of his apotheosis of feeling, he found it to be "quite ponderous," for all its foundation in "German thought and independence." This "thought" he criticized as lacking any "spontaneity or something akin to innocence and joyousness." (*SL* 18)

"Innocence" is an important value for Williams in his *Poems*. He conceives of it as having an immutable, transcendent existence. In another poem from the volume, "The Uses of Poetry" (1909), he views verse as the vehicle to reach a world where such immutability is possible. It is merely

---

[1] Williams, unpublished letters to Edgar Williams, 21 Aug. 1908, Yale Za 221. It would be five years before the museum purchased its first Cézanne, from the Armory Show.
[2] Williams, unpublished letters to Edgar Williams, 6 April 1909, Yale Za 221.

the limitations of "sense" which produce the essentially transient feelings of discord and pain.

Just like an impressionist painting which sometimes can be seen as an impression which records the transient effects of light and atmosphere. Similarly, an impressionist poetry can also be regarded as the presentation of a transient feeling of our pleasure or pain. From these aesthetics ideas of Williams' early time, we can find the young man's obvious echo to the ideas of impressionism.

Let's see a 1909 letter to Edgar, the weather in the English Channel on the voyage to Europe, Williams told his brother, exhibited the "most wonderful J. M. W. Turner skies – you know the kind with little frost-like fingers pointing at all angles for a background." There is no torrent of detail to cause the spectator "bewilderment," for the central object is isolated by a surrounding mist: "around the horizon was a transparent sunny-like mist through which the shore shone almost fairy-like, it was so silent, so dim and yet so green and white and beautiful." (*SL* 15)[1] Impressionism, as a 19th-century art movement that originated with a group of Paris-based artist, is the fountain of modern art. It plays a key role in the development of modern art, and it also brings fresh air to Williams' poetry and gives important inspiration to his poetics as well.

For Williams, the last one hundred years of French painting were an enduring inspiration, and he time and again referred to it as one of the standards of excellence in artistic expression. He believed it to have been one of the cleanest, most alert and fecund avenues of human endeavor, a positive point of intelligent insistence from which work may depart from

---

[1] Geoffrey H. Movius notes with reference to the description: "Williams had probably seen Turner's 'The Whale Ship' at the Metropolitan Museum in New York many times; and it is likely that he also knew 'The Slave Ship,' purchased by the Boston Museum of Fine Arts in 1899." "Caviar and Bread: Ezra Pound and William Carlos Williams, 1902-1914," *JML*, 5 (1976): 392.

any direction. Cézanne and Picasso (French, for Williams, because he painted in Paris) are the artists he most frequently mentioned as exemplary workers in the realm of the imagination. Demuth, Braque Duchamp and Juan Gris a number of others follow close behind.

For Williams, the poet's job was to express "the meaning of an apple," and that meaning was "not something for a child to eat or for a pie but something more closely related to Cézanne who painted them." (*Au* 31) Indeed, there are so many close connections between Williams' poetry and the visual arts. Early in 1921 he had wanted to call a collection of his poetry *Picture Poems*, changing his mind only at the last moment to have it published under the title *Sour Grapes*, a title should perhaps be seen as literally intended, and to some extend as self-deprecating (these poems are "unripe").

Almost thirty years later, during a reading at the Metropolitan Museum of Art in New York, he still saw his poems primarily as pictures:

> In the course of seeking technical improvements in the use of his medium, something he must do if he is to remain alive and effective – the artist inadvertently, perhaps, records a few pieces; portraits, landscapes or what not to please his public or patron.
>
> That's the way it has gone for the last few hundred years.
>
> Let me take advantage of this drift and present some figures of men and women to you, mostly anonymous.
>
> As T. S. Eliot said to me the only time I saw him, Williams, you've given us some good characters in your work, let's have more of them – That's what I shall follow tonight – at least at the start. You may, looking at the pictures, gather whatever there is else to find in the text as we go along.[1]

---

[1] Museum Reading,3 / 28 / 50." unpublished ms., Yale (Za Williams 174).

That Williams was not merely lured into comparisons and figures of speech by his surroundings at the time of his reading, but was moved instead by a genuine sense of solidarity with the painters whose work hung on the walls around him, can be seen from what he said to Walter Sutton in an interview which took place not long before he died. When Sutton asked him whether he and the painters spoke the same language, Williams replied: "Yes, very close – And as I've grown older, I've attempted to fuse the poetry and painting to make it the same thing –."[1] Emphasizing that design, structure, was the key to the fusion of the two media, he made it clear that for him "the meaning of the poem can be grasped by attention to the design." For Williams the identification of a poem as a composition of sharply, visually, delineated objects and events was a sufficient justification of its existence, as it is commonly accepted to be in a painting. Again it is Cézanne, an important impressionistic painter, who proves to have been the catalyst for the poet's conception of poetic structure: "I was tremendously involved in an appreciation of Cézanne. He was a designer. He put it down on the canvas so that there would be a meaning without saying anything at all. Just the relation of the parts to themselves. In considering a poem, I don't care whether it is finished or not; if it is put down with a good relation to the parts, it becomes a poem. And the meaning of the poem can be grasped by attention to the design."

Williams encountered both Demuth and Pound as a student at the University of Pennsylvania, and thus began two life-long friendships. The meeting with Demuth occurred over a dish of prunes at Mrs. Chain's boarding house on Locust Street – an incident Williams was fond of recalling. At the time Demuth was enrolled at the city's Drexel Institute,

---

[1] Walter Sutton, "A Visit with William Carlos Williams." *The Minnesota Review*, I, 3(April 1961), 109-324. Reprinted in *Interviews with William Carlos Williams: Speaking Straight Ahead*, ed. Linda Welshimer Wagner (New York Directions,1976).

transferring in 1905 to the Pennsylvania Academy of Fine Arts. Williams and Demuth were both interested in painting and literature; if Williams had repeatedly toyed with the idea of becoming a painter, Demuth could not quite make up his mind whether to become a painter or a poet until as late as 1914. Personal bonds and artistic interests in mutual interaction were to a large extent responsible for the two friends developing a very similar view of the goal of Modernism and the American scene, and for their both becoming associated with other modernist painters of their time.

In their manifesto in the first number of *Contact*, Williams and Robert McAlmon wrote: "We will be American, because we are of America... Particularly we will adopt no aggressive or inferior attitude toward 'imported thought' or art." And in a "Comment" for the second number, Williams asserted that the Americans had to become aware of their own culture, lest they "stupidly fail to learn from foreign work or stupidly swallow it without knowing how to judge its essential values."[1] This was also precisely Demuth's position. He was keenly interested in all aspects of contemporary American civilization, including those that were anathema to the defenders of a traditional "high culture". Their revolt to tradition and authorities obviously endorsed to those revolutionary ideas of the impressionist artists.

Demuth obviously shared with Williams that sharp sense of being surrounded by a larger public that was either distinctly hostile to them or not interested at all in what they were doing. But while for Williams this feeling had on the whole the effect of an additional incentive, it made Demuth often doubt whether the effort was really worthwhile. Nevertheless, in 1921 the decision was final – he would stay in America and devote himself to an art that was to be the result of the joint effort of the

---

[1] *Contact*, 1 (Dec. 1920): *Contact*, 2 (Jan. 1921): 11-12

avant-garde to respond to, and cope with, the contemporary civilization to which they belonged. The result of Demuth's decision was, among other things, a number of important paintings in oil and tempera on the landscape of the machine, and a series of "poster portraits," as he called them, done as homages to his artist friends. Almost all of these works were completed between 1920 and 1930; after that time his bad health – he suffered from diabetes – prevented him from working for a prolonged time on larger canvases.

Demuth enthusiastically endorsed Williams' college writing efforts. In a 1907 letter he declared, "I have always felt that it would happen to you some day – that you would simply have to write." (Farnham 48) Williams reciprocated with an interest in his friend's painting. In a 1956 interview he told Emily Farnham, Demuth's biographer, "Charlie gave me one of his first paintings. It was mostly yellow and lavender, a picture of a girl, and it wasn't any good. I gave it later on to Mrs. Demuth."[1] In addition to this yellow and lavender girl, Williams owned two further examples of his friend's early work. Demuth presented the watercolor *April landscape* (1911) as a wedding gift to the Williamses in 1912. Farnham describes this work as "trees treated in Impressionism manner."

Over the following twenty years Williams would come to own a number of Demuth's works, and shared ideas and friendships would be important to both of them. In 1923, when Williams published the most successful "arrangement" to come out of his interest in paintings – the poems and prose of *Spring and All* – he dedicated the book to his first artistic confidant, Demuth.

Demuth's famous homage to Williams, *I Saw the Figure 5 in Gold* (Figure 13), done in 1928, is a typical painting with some characteristics of

---

[1] Emily Farnham, "Charles Demuth, His Life, Psychology, and Works." Diss. Ohio State1959. 989.

impressionism. That Demuth based his "poster portrait" on Williams' impressionistic poem "The Great Figure" is not surprising when we recall the feeling of the poet was rooted in his common conviction that an indigenous American art had to make "contact" first and foremost with those aspects of their environment that had up to then been largely or even completely ignored. For Williams' friends, "The Great Figure" (1921), with its sensitivity to things completely outside the confines of Art, Beauty, and Culture, was a paradigmatic achievement. It was this poem in particular that Kenneth Burke singled out for praise in one of the earliest appraisals of Williams' art in 1922: "What for instance, could be more lost, more uncorrelated, a closer Contact, a great triumph of anti-culture, than this poem." (Burke 50)

> Among the rain
> and lights
> I saw the figure 5
> in gold
> on a red
> firetruck
> moving
> tense
> unheeded
> to gong clangs
> siren howls
> and wheels rumbling
> through the dark city. (*CP I* 174)

In this poem, the image of the firetruck racing through the city in the midst of the frenzy of "going clangs" and "siren howls" evokes the enthusiasm of the impressionist for the dynamic chaos of the modern urban civilization. "The Great Figure" is one of the poems that recall impressionists' influence, in particular that of the relationship between man and environment. The golden figure 5 is a veritable object discovered by the poet among the innumerable things that belong to the neglected "soulless" present-day technological environment so systematically bypassed by the more traditional artists. The impressionist ideas undoubtedly helped Williams to come to the conviction that a poem, like any other work of art , "can be made of anything"[1] The very title of "The Great Figure" contains this conviction in a nutshell: In 1920, when the poem was published for the first time, a reader probably expected it to be about a figure of public importance rather than about a number, or immediately realized the clash between what one could generally expect to find in poetry and what one found here – a poem that violated the basic poetic conventions by almost any standard.

Just like an impressionistic picture which records merely the impression of transient feelings of us, when the readers finish reading the poem, the dramatic moment is over, with the firetruck disappearing into the night. Thus the last line of the poem takes us back to the beginning; the poem opens and closes with a wide-angle shot, so to speak, of the dark city with its rain and lights, a background which very effectively frames the sudden appearance of the golden figure in an exciting flash of color, sound, and movement.

If "The Great Figure" is one of Williams' most memorable and delightful early poems, the painting by Demuth which it inspired is undoubtedly one of the artist's masterpieces. *I Saw the Figure 5 in Gold* is the last and most famous of his "poster portraits." Demuth obviously tried

---

[1] *Imaginations*, ed. Webster Schott (New York, 1970), 70.

to render as dramatically as possible the sudden appearance, the dramatic impression of the 5 that looms large before the eye for a moment before the red firetruck vanishes into the night and darkness. This led to the daring and ingenious idea of painting the 5 three times. The largest figure, filling the whole canvas, seems to float in the air right before our eyes; the second and third recede into the background, drawing the eye to the center and creating a sense of rapid motion and the depth of space into which the firetruck and the 5 disappear.

The basic aims of Demuth's picture were the same as those of Williams' poem – they were meant to be a reflection of the contemporary American scene, an expression, ideally, of an essential aspect of the world in which the artists lived and with which they had to cope. Both Williams and Demuth were convinced that this was a world that would not and should not, emulate the more refined and/or more decadent culture of Europe, a world, however, that had a vitality all its own, and offered many new, unexpected beauties.

In Williams' *Spring and All*, dedicated to Demuth, we find not only the same basic device of juxtaposition but even the same clashes between the natural and the industrial, the organic and the mechanistic, the sublime and the banal, the religious and the secular, the idealistic and the vitalistic. And in Williams' poems, too, the relation between the juxtaposed realms and their respective values is highly complex; the reader approaching them with too simplistic a scheme of values will be unable to term with them. The mind has to abandon the traditional categories, so as to prevent to slip into the old mode.

The fact that Williams' urban landscape poems and Demuth's paintings are in many ways related to impressionism. They are obvious, when we compare Demuth's landscapes to the impressionistic poems. Both the poet and the painter create a field of action, as we have seen, by a series interacting elements – elements that create tension or conflict by clashing with one another, or fuse with others to create harmony.

2.2   Pound's Influence on Williams in Visual Arts

William Carlos Williams knew Ezra Pound, a vivid mentor of him, from the time they were both undergraduate students at the University of Pennsylvania in the early years of the 20th century. Pound soon went abroad for an almost permanent residence in England and then on the Continent; Williams (partly educated in Europe as a child) was content to revisit Europe, but for the most part stayed at home after taking his medical degree at Pennsylvania in 1906. Williams' early verse was somewhat derivative, although he was almost at once quite modern, with his friends, the imagists. In 1917, with the rather experimental *Al Que Quiere!*, Williams shows that he was finding his own way. From that time forth, in both poetry and prose, he spoke with his own distinctive voice. And it was a distinctive American voice. Ezra Pound, in a 1928 essay, suggested that Williams was discovering his native country virtually with the eyes of an outsider.

When Pound wrote to Williams in 1908 defending his *A Lume Spento* from his friend's charge of "poetic anarchy," he called Williams attention to "what the poets and musicians and painters are doing with a good deal of convention that has masqueraded as law" (Witemeyer 8). Pound's letter give evidence of what he was gaining from an interest in the painters: he scoffs at the demands of "the public," dismisses the traditional subject matter of verse, and declares "sometimes I use rules of Spanish, Anglo-Saxon and Greek metric that are not common in the English of Milton's or Miss Austin's day" (Witemeyer 29). The modernist painters had already, by this date, developed similar strategies for painting. In fact, the "law" that painters such as Cézanne, Whistler and Kandinsky had challenged covered almost every aspect of their art. The modernist poets were also drawn to the strategies of the painters by the nature of the modernist poetic. This part deals largely with Williams' response to Pounds' work and to the magazines associated with Pound.

Before his first trip to Europe in 1908, Pound had encountered a number of minor American painters. Among these were William Brooke Smith, to whom *A Lume Spento* is dedicated, Fred Reed Whiteside in Philadelphia, and Fred Nelson Vance in Crawfordsville, Indiana. When he returned to the United States for seven months in June 1910, his painter associates in New York were Carlton Gliddens, Warren Dahler, and Yeats's father Jack B. Yeats.[①]

Writing from New York in 1911, he told his parents to "read 'The New Art in Paris' in the February *Forum*. There is an answer to a number of things. That ought to prove my instinct for where I can breathe. It's mostly news to me, but of the right sort."[②] The article was written by Stieglitz's associate Marius De Zayas. De Zayas praises the receptivity of the Parisian audience to art which it does not initially understand – an atmosphere Pound would certainly appreciate.

When Pound was in Paris, he told his mother that he had visited the studio of a "brand new painter," and that he had "seen a number of Cézanne pictures in a private gallery." He visited the Salon Des Independents, declaring "Matisse's one canvas is well painted," although "freaks there are in abundance."[③] The note of skepticism is sounded again in his late 1911

---

① Vance and Whiteside appear in Pound's "Redondillas, or Something of That Sort" (1911).
   I praise God for a few royal fellows
   like Piarr and Fred Vance and Whiteside
   Pound, *Collected Early Poems*, 216. Vance also appears in the first version of Canto Ⅱ, *Poetry*. 10 (1917): 187-188.
② Pound, Ezra. unpublished letters to Isabel Pound, 1911. Paige Carbons, Yale.
③ Pound, Ezra. unpublished letters to Isabel Pound, 26 March 1911: 16 May 1911: to Homer Pound, May 1911, Paige Carbons, Yale.

essay series "I Gather the Limbs of Osiris," There he found the contemporary arts "damned and clogged by the mimetic," noting that many of "the painters of the moment escape through eccentricity."[1]

In his famous 1913 essay "A Few Don'ts by an Imagiste" Pound defined an "Image" as "that which presents an intellectual and emotional complex in an instant of time."[2] Whistler's pictures invited apprehension in a single instant in terms of the artist's imposition of form, and the imagist poem offered the poet one way to write such a "complex." Through control of form, painting or poetry could manifest a way of seeing – recording the conscious purpose of the artist, and not his enslavement to traditional modes of expression.

Reviewing Williams's second published volume, *The Tempers*, in the London Journal *The New Freewoman* in December 1913, Pound read his friend as engaged in a similar strategy. Williams "makes a bold attempt to express himself directly and convinces one that the emotions he feels are veritably his own." He noted "the effect of color…the particularly vivid and rich range of colour in which his emotions seem to present themselves, 'gold against blue,' to his vision."[3] For Pound, the impulse behind Williams's work is an emotion apprehended visually.

In this same year Pound discussed the germination of his "In a Station of the Metro" (the concluding poem of the "Contemporania" series).

> The apparition of these faces in the crowd:
> Petals on a wet, black bough.

For this account, in *T.P.'s Weekly*, the poem is related to Japanese tradition," where a work of art is not estimated by its acreage."[4] But a

---

[1] Pound, Ezra. "I Gather the Limbs of Ostris," *The New Age*. 22 Feb, 1912, 393; *Selected Prose*. 42.
[2] Pound, Ezra. "A Few Don'ts by an Imagiste." *Poetry*, 1 (1913): 200; *Literary Essays of Ezra Pound*. ed. T. S. Eliot (London: Faber,1954), 4.
[3] Pound, Ezra. "The Tempers," *The New Freewoman*. 1 (1913): 227.
[4] Pound, Ezra. "How I Began." *T. P.'s Weekly*, 6 June 1913: 143.

year later his description of translating a pattern of color into a verbal image is retold around a critical apparatus a good deal more painterly. Although the emotion originally appeared to him in terms of a pattern of color, being a poet, not a painter, he sought an "image" to express that emotion where a painter would have recorded the colors. "The image is the poet's pigment: with that in mind you can go head and apply Kandinsky, you can transpose his chapter on the language of form and colour and apply it to the writing of verse."[1]

Many new art ideas were introduced to Pound, and to England, by T. E. Hulme. Pound wrote to his mother on 20 January 1914, "Hulme lectured at the QUEST last night on futurism and post-impressionism, followed by fervent harangues from Wyndham Lewis and myself."[2] What Hulme actually lectured on was Worringer's aesthetics. His talk survives as "Modern Art and its Philosophy" collected in *Speculations*, much of the argument, as he confesses, "practically an abstract of Worringer's views."[3]

Pound reported on the Quest meeting for *Egoist* readers on 16 February 1914, and summarized a number of Hulme's points. He describes Hulme's lecture as "almost wholly unintelligible," but this is sarcasm directed at the audience, not Hulme. Pound clearly found it intelligible, and concludes "Mr. Hulme was quite right in saying that the difference between the new art and the old was not a difference in degree but a difference in kind: a difference in intention." He echoes Hulme's choice of artists, "Epstein is the only sculptor in England" (although he finds Gaudier-Brzeska also worthy of note).

---

[1] Pound, Ezra. "Vorticism." Fortnightly Review, 1 Sept. 1914, 461-471; reprinted in Gaudier-Brzeska (1916: New York: New Directions,1970),81-94.
[2] Pound, Ezra. unpublished letter to Isabel Pound, 20 Jan 1914, Paige Carbons, Yale.
[3] T. E. Hulme, "Modern Art and Its Phylisophy," *Speculations*, ed. Herbert Read (New York: Harcourt, Brace, 1924).82.

Chapter 2
Influences of Visual Arts on Williams

Pound's own talk – described in his report as given by "a third speaker" – discusses the "two totally opposed theories of aesthetic" that come from either regarding art as passive acceptance of sensations, or "as an instrument for carrying out the decrees of the will (or the soul)" – Kandinsky's word – "or whatever you wish to term it." This art of the "will" is essentially undemocratic, the artist taking no more heed of "general franchise" than he does of conventional form.[1]

For Pound, the modern poet was in a disharmony with his immediate surroundings that made him kin to those artists of past and present whose similar disjunction produced their abstract art. This hostile environment often appears in Pound's poems of these years as the philistine literary establishment of editors, academics, and febrile writers who threaten the livelihood and work of the genuine artist. In poems such as "Et Faim Sallir les Loups des Boys" the isolation is presented dramatically.

> I cling to the spar,
> Washed with the cold salt ice
> I cling to the spar –
> Insidious modern waves, civilization,
> Civilized hidden snares.

Williams followed the ferment of ideas in London as he moved towards his poetic independence with the New York / New Jersey "Others" group. In 1912 Pound sent him the new Chicago *Poetry*, advising him to subscribe, and in the same year dedicated the volume *Ripostes* to him. In 1913 he arranged for the publication of Williams's *The Tempers* with Elkin

---

[1] Pound, Ezra. "The New Sculpture." The Egoist,1(1914): 67-68.

Matthews in London. Writing to Williams at the end of this year, he told him to subscribe to *The Egoist* and to watch out for "the coming sculptor, Gaudier-Brzeska."[1] He included Williams in the imagist anthologies *Des Imagistes* (1914) and *Catholic Anthology* (1915).

In *Poetry* and *The Egoist* Williams followed the outpourings of imagist verse and critiques, telling his friend Viola Jordan in June 1914 that he was himself an imagist, and that she was underestimating the worth of *The Egoist*. In telling her to read that month's *poetry* for Ford Maddox Ford's "On Heaven" he implied his agreement with the view of Pound and Richard Aldington that the work was the finest yet to emerge from the new movement.[2]

When Pound moved from imagism to vorticism, making imagism, according to F. S. Flint, "to mean pictures as Wyndham Lewis understands them,"[3] Williams responded with similar experiments. His poems in *The Tempers* follow Pound in evincing a nostalgia for past eras when the importance of poetry was clearly manifest, but as Pound developed a strategy for bringing the "energized past" to bear upon the concerns of the modern poet, so the note of nostalgia disappears in Williams' work. A number of his poems from these years demonstrate this interest in the cycles of art as they are discussed in the work of Pound, Hulme, and Gaudier-Brzeska. Past models of geometrical art are brought into poems that map out a strategy for the contemporary expression of the poet's America.

---

[1] Pound, Ezra. unpublished letter to William Carlos Williams, 26 Oct. 1912, Poetry Collection of the Lockwood Memorial Library, SUNY buffalo, F501: Pound, Letters, 27.
[2] Williams, unpublished letters to Viola Jordan, 7 June 1914, 11 June 1914, Viola Baxter Jordan Papers, Beinecke Rare Book and Manuscript Library, Yale.
[3] F. S. Flint. "The History of Imagism." The Egoist, 2 (1915): 70.

In Williams' 1916 "Metric Figure" describes the new movements in art as revelatory of form.

> Veils of clarity
>
> have succeeded
>
> veils of color (*CP I* 51)

Color, as Kandinsky argued in his analysis of its effects, should be a directed, knowledgeable application of the primary elements of painterly self-expression. Through the sensitive appreciation of its intrinsic qualities, color is to be utilized as carefully as any other formal element in art. Color is revelatory of form, not bound to conventional representations of nature. In "La Flor" (1914) it is Williams' praise of Pound over "versifiers" that "his verse is crimson when they speak of the rose," and he contrasts Pound with "Those who bring their ingenious tapestries to such soft perfection / Borrowing majesty from a true likeness to natural splendour,"[1] In Williams' "Metric Figure" (1916),

> Veils of clarity
>
> have succeeded
>
> veils of color
>
> that wove
>
> as the sea
>
> sliding above
>
> submerged whiteness.

---

[1] The Egoist, 1 (1914): 308; New Directions 16, (New York: New Directions, 1957), 10-11.

Veils of clarity

reveal sand

glistening –

falling away

to an edge –

sliding

beneath the advancing ripples. (*CP I* 51-52)

On one level the poem presents sunrise, but on another it describes the shift from impressionism to the hard edged geometrics of modernist art. Changes in poetry – from atmospheric verse to the "clarity" of imagism – have accompanied the developments in the visual arts. The "veils of color" that informed impressionist work have given way to the controlling clarity of an art that reveals "an edge." The light and sea are now "advancing" instead of "sliding," while the revealed matter of art falls away toward its expressive angularity – its edge.

In his essays, Williams' definition of a work of art could apply to the strategy behind his early poems.

Life that is here and now is timeless. That is the universal I am seeking: to embody that in a work of art, a new world that is always "real."

All things otherwise grow old and rot. By long experience the only thing that remains unchanged and unchangeable is the work of art. It is because of the element of timelessness in it, its sensuality. The only world that exists is the world of senses. The world of the artist. (*SE* 196)

Chapter 2
Influences of Visual Arts on Williams

In his whole lifetime, Williams continued to experiment with strategies of modern art. Pound had directed Williams to the ideas coming out of that contemporary European consciousness, but now Williams had to place an American stamp upon those ideas. In meeting the "Others" group, and Marsden Hartley, in the years after 1914, he joined other American artists similarly groping both for an individual and a national voice within the international upheaval in the arts.

Chapter 3

The Observer and the Observed as Co-maker in Williams' Poetics

"Impressionism suggests impressionistic artwork is the interplay between the observer and the observed, and it concerns the observers' mental process on the object" (Nagel 21). The contact between mind and thing (through the agency of the senses) is justly advocated in Williams' poetics. Very briefly, contact may be thought of as the connection between self and thing, between the internal mind and the external world (Ostrom 13). From Williams' poetic perspective, readers' (or observers') experience completes the artwork, since he leaves the reader (or the observer) with his own imagination devices to determine what the reality is. Impressionist tendencies in the poetic world of William Carlos Williams are explored in this chapter.

3.1   The Interplay of the Observer and the Observed

In April 1874, Claude Monet showed *Impression, Sunset* at an exhibition. This was the first of what we now know as the impressionist exhibitions. Monet's painting and its eccentric title helped give impressionism its name and, indeed, for many people, have come to exemplify impressionism in general. It is incontestable that the concept of the impression was of central importance to a good deal of impressionist practice. However, there was a more positive dimension to the term which influenced Monet's choice of it. It implied that to paint in such a way was to be sincere or honest to the appearance of a motif under a single, unified light. In his painting, Monet was clearly interested in recording how light and atmosphere alter the appearance of a motif as they change during the course of the day. It seems to have been the case that in painting an impression, an artist was trying to record how the atmosphere effect of a particular moment produced a particular impression on him or her as an individual. When a painter saw a landscape at a single glance, he translated it in his own manner, while keeping its truth and also communicating the emotion he felt. Here, everything is original, the craftsmanship and the impression. The foundation on which this concept of the impression rested was that of Positivist philosophy. The Positivists argued that an impression was subjective in two senses: it belonged to the consciousness of the individual who experienced it and hence was not an accurate account of the reality. But more importantly, they argued that an impression took a form unique to the individual having it; because every individual was made differently, and because every individual brought her or his personal stock of memories, associations, and feelings to what she or he saw. To sum up, when the impressionists spoke of their interest in impressions, they meant they were interested in painting the unique effect that nature produced in them, or the experience that marked the meeting place of the individual, interior self and the outside world. Most importantly, when they claimed to paint their impressions, they implied they were recording the primal impact nature made on their senses, or the raw, unarticulated appearance things had when seen without prejudice.

Many paintings of impressionists position the observer in a particular physical and psychological relationship to the scene they depict. They present the scene through the eyes of a casual man of leisure and ask the observer to see it through the same eyes. They contain what has been called an "observer in the picture," and cohere only when the real observer imaginatively "becomes" this other character. Often paintings of this type identify the character and position of the observer in the picture by very carefully specifying where they are painted and sometimes, as with Edquard Manet, they have figures within the painting which look back out of it and further identify the observer in the picture in this way. A picture, Auguste Renoir's *The Umbrella* (1881-1885, Figure 2) deals in great deal with the frisson of being observed. In it, the observer is positioned as man in a fashionable park, or at least the way the observer's attention is engaged by the attractive young woman at the left of the painting suggests this. This woman is carrying a basket covered with an oilskin, perhaps because it contains perishable goods or flowers to sell, and her dress shows she is of a lower social class than the well-dressed people who populate the rest of the picture. The picture is designed to prompt the observer into imagining himself making an advance to the girl – he might offer her his umbrella, for instance, since it has started to rain and she has no protection. However, we can assume there is something illicit in the observer's intentions because he is being watched by the little girl in the foreground with a hoop. What is more, she is being watched by her mother; who in turn appears to be under observation by the man at the left of the painting – perhaps the father of the family, or a potential rival for the younger woman. Accordingly, if the observer is to make an illicit advance to the woman with the basket he must do this without attracting attention; crucially, he must do it before the little girl's mother follows the direction of her child's gaze and alerts the man at the left of the painting as to the observer's intentions. In other words, the picture trades on contemporary anxieties about the necessity of weighing up a situation and acting quickly in order to evade detection by one's peers. Paintings of this sort suggest that the observer's vision was marked by a sense of loss. Not only do situations and events threaten to happen too quickly to hold on to, but even love at first sight threatens to be no more than love at last sight as well. It is no surprise, therefore, that "a desire to give the transitory moment some fixity and accessibility is one of the recurrent features of impressionism" (Konnegger 51).

The impressionists of painting and literature share an interest in subjective perception. A similar relativism links both arts at the general level, as well, as each abandons faith in larger systems in favor of faith in what seems personally true (Matz 45). "An impression is personal, but universal – subjective, but not therefore wholly idiosyncratic – and falls somewhere between analytic scrutiny and imaginative invention" (Matz 16). This in-betweenness is essential. An impression is never simply a feeling, a thought, or a sensation. It partakes, rather, of a mode of experience that is neither sensuous nor rational, neither felt nor thought, but somewhere in between. Belonging to none of these categories, an impression similarly belongs to no one theoretical way of thinking. "Impressionist style refers to a manner of suggesting reality. According to the impressionist writers, reality is an interplay of the individual's consciousness and the surrounding world" (Konnegger 13).

Adapting this heightened consciousness to the new reality of objects means fusing the inner ego with the outer world. This phenomenological relationship underlies the entire vision and aesthetic of impressionism. The impressionist writers share with recent investigators in phenomenology the conviction that "we can not know reality independently of consciousness, and that we cannot know consciousness independently of reality" (Stowell 32).

Impressionism is born from the fundamental insight that our consciousness is sensitive and passive. Man's consciousness faces this world as pure passivity, a mirror in which the world inscribes or reflects itself. As a detached spectator, the individual considers the world without having a standpoint in it. Reality is a synthesis of sense-impressions. Impressionist art suggests an emotional reality.

> No longer is there a separation between subject and object, nor is one given precedence over the other. Reality is the synthesis of perceiver and perceived – each exists and each creates meaning for the other. The new aesthetic is based upon integrated juxtaposition, upon a gestalt: the perceiver superimposes on an object actual physical qualities based upon his own memory, mood, and perspective; the object takes on and reflects the physical properties of the surrounding environment; the object and its reflections simultaneously infuse the perceiver's own set of physical and psychological characteristics. (Stowell 32)

"Impressionism means a new attitude toward life" (Konnegger 14). Can we forget to "know" that the cloud is white, the tree is green; and to feel, say, paint or express what the eye actually "sees"? What we actually see is a vibration of light on matter in dissolution. To make it simple and clear, to impressionists, reality involves two aspects: the inner world and the outside world. The literary writers conveys us what he observes from the outside world. His writing includes two aspects: the observer, the writer himself (or the narrator) and the observed, the object. The formation of impression depends on the illusion of the observer and an object capability of being made present to senses. "The fusion of the individual's consciousness with the world creates a unity between visual appearance and mental reality. Reality, then, is seen as a harmony of illusion and reality" (Konnegger 38).

Chapter 3
The Observer and the Observed as Co-maker in Williams' Poetics

The general device used by impressionist writers to create an impressionistic world and to express impressionist ideas is in one sense the most crucial, for it is the one that makes the other function in the capacities assigned them. Reader must employ his imagination (or his illusion), and must participate in the creative act. In the impressionist writing the role of reader as co-maker is especially important, for then the reader experiences directly the impressionistic nature of the characters' world. By participating with the characters in their experiences and thoughts the reader learns with them about their world and even goes beyond them, for he participates through several consciousnesses. This multiple perspective which synthesizes the possibilities of perception enables the writer to escape the limitations a single view naturally imposes, and allows him (or her) a broad spectrum from which to draw his (or her) personal vision. As a modernist poet favoring painting from his childhood, William Carlos Williams was unavoidably influenced by the modernist ideas of impressionist in his early time. Let's take Williams' early poem, "The Rose" (1923), as an example:

> The rose is obsolete
> but each petal ends in
> an edge, the double facet
> cementing the grooved
> columns of air – The edge
> cuts without cutting
> meets – nothing – renews
> itself in metal or porcelain –

Williams translates the tactile reality of the rose into words which by the very intensity of their tactile associations force us to consider the rose

completely in terms of the actual existence it represents, rather than allowing us to give it a metaphorical, or otherwise literary "significance":

> Somewhere the sense
> makes copper roses
> steel roses –

And:

> From the petal's edge a line starts
> that being of steel
> infinitely fine, infinitely
> rigid penetrates
> the Milky Way
> without contact – lifting
> from it – neither hanging
> nor pushing –
>
> The fragility of the flower
> unbruised
> penetrates space.

The fact is that Williams in his poem succeeded to a large extent in avoiding a discursive personal interpretation of the "meaning"of the work. This leaves the observer (or we say the reader) free to interpret that perception according to his own patterns of visual understanding, without having to adjust himself through an enforced meaning to the artist's obstructive intellectualization of his initial and all-important subconscious understanding. Williams wishes the observer to see the observed (or we say "that work") through the particular selection of his eyes, but allows us to develop our own understanding of the visual construct which constitutes his poem. Williams breaks away from description to direct interpretation: first when he begins by saying that "the rose is obsolete," and second when he asserts that

> The rose carried weight of love
> but love is at an end – of roses
>
> It is at the edge of the
> petal that love waits (*CP I* 195-196)

But both instances of Williams' interpretive interference are minor, and not sufficiently specific to restrict the focus of the reader's personal intuitive apprehension. Williams, in other words, has left the poem, "Sharper, neater, more cutting / figured in majolica – ," to "the broken plate / glazed with a rose." (*CP I* 196) By reading this poem, we can find that we ourselves (or the readers) actually participate in the creation of the artwork, that is to say the observer and the observed worked as co-maker in this artwork.

Impressionist ideas can be found in many of Williams' early poetry. Moreover, one important point should be mentioned is that impressionism also provides very important inspiration to the young poet for his later establishment of his own quite special poetics, which influenced his style of writing all his lifetime and also influenced lots of Williams' followers. It is known to us that Williams' poetry plays a key role in the development of American modernist poetry. His poems are always thought too fresh and somewhat difficult for his readers to understand. Therefore, a further exploration of Williams' poetics will give his readers a key to disclose the secret in his unique poems. In the following part, several early poems of Williams are given as examples to discuss an important impressionistic character, the harmony interplay of the illusion and the reality in Williams' poetics.

3.2 A Harmony of Illusion and Reality in Williams' Poetics

Williams' poetic world is as diverse as the actual. The true focus of his attention is men. Even as a matter of simple statistical fact, his most often used material is people, and people are the ones he sees in the everyday world about him. "All of Williams' work is his complex of ideas about the nature of art and art's relation to the well-being of both the individual and society" (Ostrom 4). Art for art's sake is for him an unintelligible statement, only for man's sake must art exist. The spirit bearing it, its origin and its end, must be its intention for men's use. In his typically American way, Williams has worked against the American popular tradition that art is by definition useless – at best a luxury, at worst an escape from the pressures of actuality – and therefore separated from, and opposed to, the "practical" and the "useful. He desires to establish the poem as a weapon in the daily battle. The purpose of his poems is to be useful. He will make available his understanding of what is man's place in the world: what are man's relationships to other men and what are his relationships to the other, nonhuman things. He will illuminate the dark areas of men's existence. And whatever in the poem does not deal with men directly, but presents the nonhuman – this will be an illumination of men too, for this is that physical, actual world, or part of it, in which they live. It is not a simply intellectual power that makes the poem for him an indispensable condition of life; it is, as he has said, the poems' rootedness in the physical world of actuality. His poetry is the proper statement of his quality: "No ideas but in things."

"For Williams, there are three modes of being: (1) that which we perceive with the senses (actuality), (2) that which is but may be unperceived (reality), and (3) that which we wish (ideality)" (Ostrom 16). The differentiation of reality from actuality is the most to make, since one is always involved in the process of everyday experience; but for this very reason it is also the most important to the reader as a source of useful knowledge in the poem. That is to say, it is Williams' contention that the world as we know it is often a distortion of the world as it exists objectively, independent of our understanding of it: not only is the extent of our knowledge at best incomplete, but within that partial body are illusions that we mistake for truth (Ostrom 17–19). However, the only way to reach reality, he believes, is through actuality: "no ideas but in things" is the credo of a poet who knows that we do indeed live in a place where we must deal with what is about us. The world of theory, of hypothesis and idealization, has, and can have, no existence of its own, apart from what we bump into every day. Reality is expressible only in the things, the actuality, of our world. Very similar to the impressionist writers, Williams rejected the traditional emphasis upon order, thought, and clearness. In his whole lifetime, Williams seeks constantly for those infrequent images of the poet's perception which can show illusion and reality in harmony. In a poem for which he is best probably known, "The Red Wheelbarrow" (though it is really only a section of the long poem "Spring and All", 1923), he gives merely the briefest possible account of his data; except for one word at the outset that indicates his intent, he leaves the actual world intact for the reader's interpretation.

> so much depends
>
> upon
>
> a red wheel
>
> barrow

glazed with rain

water

beside the white

chickens (*CP I* 224)

Williams is attempting to teach by showing and to make the reader learn by doing. He would not think of asking complete acquiescence and unthinking reverence on the reader's part for the "authority" of the printed word. True education is for him not a mere process of memorization of the abstractions of a complex intellectual construction; his low valuation of the purely rational process of "knowing" makes that an impossibility. Rather, it is comprised of a knowledge and understanding through the imagination, both the individual parts of one's vision of reality and of their relationships as the pieces show themselves in the actual world. For this reason Williams is forever saying, in effect, "Look at this and see how important it is – and how (why) it is important to the wholeness of the world" (*SE* 43). "The Red Wheelbarrow" is the prime example of this idea. In terms of both his actual world and the poem's world, wheelbarrow is indispensable if their wholeness is to be kept; remove it, and you remove one point where the human, the natural, and the mechanical worlds meet in harmony, where the wheelbarrow, its implied user, the chickens, and possibly even the rain have that quality-in-common for which Williams (like ourselves) is always seeking so that he may at last form a paradigm – minute, perhaps, but of infinite worth – of the true order of our world. Remove the wheelbarrow, he says, and you remove one of the few measurable, knowable points of reference and fragment the whole into illusorily separated orders (Ostrom 69).

This brief poem is a good example of how, more than anyone else in modern American poetry, Williams has brought attention to the things of our world. By insisting upon "no ideas but in things" he has forced his readers to discard their assumptions about the world, assumptions, for the most part, that permit men to avoid having to look at things; he has forced them to examine the objects in his poems for what they are in themselves, not for what they represent. In this respect Williams differs considerably from T. S. Eliot. In his statement about the "objective correlative," Eliot said:

> The only way of expressing emotion in the form of art is by finding an "objective correlative"; in other words, a set of objects, a situation, a chain of events which shall be the formula of that particular emotion; such that when the external facts, which must terminate in sensory experience, are given, the emotion is immediately evoked. (Eliot 124-125)

Obviously, this is a demand for a form of symbolism; Eliot is not concerned about what actuality is given so long as some actuality is given. What is important is the emotion (or in some cases the idea) that the physical objects or actions refer to. But unlike Eliot's symbolic peach (or hotels, oystershells, fog, and so forth) in "The Love Song of J. Alfred Prufrock," Williams' red wheelbarrow, rain, and white chickens are there because they actually are there in our everyday world, our experience. It is certain that as typical objects they contain implicit extensions of meaning; but these extensions inhere in the realities of the things themselves and in their place in our experience. "The Red Wheelbarrow" provides a fresh view of reality in the perception of the previously unseen relationship. This poem speaks for much of Williams' poetry, which expresses close, intimate contact with the material, physical world.

At a virtual beginning of Williams' career (1917) Ezra Pound wrote to him in a now famous letter:

I was very glad to see your wholly incoherent un-American poems in the L. R. (*Little Review*)

Of course Sandburg will tell you that you miss the "Big drifts," and Bodenheim will object to your not being sufficiently decadent.

(You thank your bloomin gawd you've got enough Spanish blood to muddy up your mind, and prevent the current American ideation from going through it like a blighted colander.)

The thing that saves your work is *opacity*, and don't you forget it. Opacity is NOT an American quality. Fizz, swish, gabble of verbiage, these are echt Amerikanisch. (*SLP&W* 31)

The opacity to which Pound was referring is not, however, the sort produced by a poet's having and using a greater range of knowledge and reference than the reader can come by even with moderate difficulty – that is to say, the sort we found in Pound's own work or in T. S. Eliot's. Actually, it is Williams' unwillingness to spell out for the reader what the poem ought to mean; it is his determination to make the poem a replica of the actual world from which the reader may learn, by use of the imagination (or we say the illusion) what complexities underlie the "simplicity" of the materials. Like the world it reflects, the poem is only partly revealed. One typical example of this opacity is "The Bull" (1922).

It is in captivity –
ringed, haltered, chained
to a drag
the bull is godlike

Unlike the cows

he lives alone, nozzles

the sweet grass gingerly

to pass the time away

He kneels, lies down

and stretching out

a foreleg licks himself

about the hoof

then stays

with half-closed eyes,

Olympian commentary on

the bright passage of days.

In an impressionistic literature work, the impressionist writers always manage to make the authorial presence remain hidden and allow the characters to exist and to experience for themselves. From this the reader must develop his own understanding, just as he does in actual life. Here Williams' fundamental intent is hidden in the virtually perfect unity of the poem as we see it: as it stands, it is a clear picture of a minute corner of the natural world. But what we see as actuality is merely the revealed part of a larger, implied structure. The foundation for the poem – its hidden mass – is Williams' complex of ideas about wholeness and divorce, and thus about good and evil, as well as his desire to show (teach) us the relationship of reality to appearance.

– The round sun

smooths his lacquer

through
the glossy pinetrees

his substance hard
as ivory or glass –
through which the wind
yet plays –

        Milkless

he nods
the hair between his horns
and eyes matted
with hyacinthine curls (CP I 240)

What strikes one immediately about the poem is its quietness. The explosion that seems imminent in the first statement of the bull's captivity never takes place; instead, the poem grows increasingly static as the bull's passivity becomes more and more obviously the focus of Williams' concern Usually the epitome of raw, wild, passionate strength, the bull here seems, on the contrary, rather like a magnificent huge porcelain figure, removed from us and from all the living world of actuality. He is as Williams says "godlike." But in his separation from the cows he has been emasculated – "ringed, haltered, chained / to a drag"; his appearance has been made more perfect, but his purpose (which is to say the reality of his existence) has been perverted. In his sequestration, the bull is an image of the male-principle divorced from the female-principle that it complements and is meant to fecundate.

Seen even in the most literal way, the poem is thus more than one thing: it is a replica of the actual world in which we see the bull foe what it is, hard, strong, remote, useless alone, yet beautiful in those qualities; it is an exposition of the perversion of things by divorce and of the evil inherent in such perversion; and by implication it is a statement of the natural wholeness of things, here in terms of sexuality. However, we may consider the bull not merely in its own being, but as a typical example, a paradigm of all things partaking of the male-principle. From the bull's being "ringed, haltered, chained / to a drag" as contrasted to the inherent freedom of the imagination; from its sequestration – its useless (a perversion of reality) and divorce from the sensual world; and from its milklessness, implying an inability to sustain life in others, and its ivory or glass-like hardness, implying the absence of life itself – from all this it is possible to infer that Williams associates the male-principle essentially with the rational faculties and, by logical antithesis, the female with the imaginative. What Williams sees, then, in the female-principle is evidently the combination of productiveness (perhaps more properly reproductiveness – the power of maintaining life), acceptance, and gentleness. Maleness and femaleness, violence and gentleness are a part of actual world. It is the ordering of the violence of the world we live in that makes us whole. Art establishes orders by means of the imagination, and, maintaining wholeness, it produces those ideas-in-things that Williams believes the only truly useful information for ordering the actions – which is to say, for the government – of men's lives. And it is love, the source of ideal direct contact between people, that makes their personal relationship whole. In a word, Williams' ultimate reference for sexuality is to the problem of "divorce" in our world and its effect upon us. Sex is the appropriate link between the human and the natural world. Where sex is normal, it unites the human and the natural in an image of harmony. But where it is perverted, it becomes a sign of "divorce".

The life-urge, the avidity for all experience – is a constantly repeated concept in Williams' poems. We find sometimes that for all his writing of the natural world, his world – his concern – is fundamentally human. For all that flowers are frequently the materials of his poems – and used with such skill that they seem all his interest – his intent is for the most part that we compare them with our human realm, so often fragmented and perverted from its own natural course. For in his judgment of the world, the great tragedy of our lives is our isolation, our maddening inability in the midst of men to make satisfactory contact with others. If we must take peace with our physical environment, as he says, we must do so because it will help us to find our common humanity and make peace with ourselves. Love takes on in his poems additional meanings as the prime motive force in the world, it becomes significant of the acceptance of life, of experience, because it is the most elemental, most intimate and direct mode of making contact with the life that is outside us. Williams' insistence upon love's centrality to our lives is thus a desperate plea for a more constant, deeper, and more openly direct contact between men, and between men and the natural world.

Perhaps of all the major modernists, Williams was willing to let things speak for themselves, to bridge the gap between the self and the world. While Williams appreciates the independent status of nature, he intuits a larger unity embracing both man and nature – a unity that the imagination can grasp and, in so doing, can also grasp values which are potentially present in things. Recognizing the independence of nature frees and encourages the poet to find his own independence, not by trying to copy the external forms but by imitating the inner creative energies behind the appearances of nature. Or as Williams says, it is only through the imagination that a work of art "escapes plagiarism after nature and becomes a creation."[1] Williams' poetry celebrates an interchange between mind and nature, an experience in which the barrier between inner and outer worlds seems to be overcome. This kind of mind-matter relationship, common to romantic poets, was most strikingly formulated by an early progenitor of romantic thought, the German idealist F. W. Schelling:

> If consciousness were something absolutely inward and no unmediated contact between it and outward things could be conceived, we would find that we do not at all see things outside of us... but that we simply see them in ourselves. If this were so, there could be no possible separation between inner and outer worlds. And since inner is only distinguishable in contrast to outer, the inner along with the outer world would unavoidably collapse. (Markos 35)

The passage first emphasizes that consciousness is not "absolutely inward," but is spread outward, occupying, so to speak, the same space as things themselves. Such interpenetration of mind and thing, a basic premise of organicism, makes possible an "unmediated contact" with external reality. Through sensory experience (man's sensory perception in Williams' words), Williams opens a new relationship with the everyday world.

3.3　"Glass" Poetry: A Case Study on Williams' Poetics

Since the image of "glass" appears frequently in Williams' poetry in his early time, critics name them Williams' "glass" poetry. In one sense, the alignment between painting frames and window frames is unremarkable.

---

[1] Imaginations, ed. Webster Schott (New York, 1970), 111. Contains Kara in Kell: Improvisations (1920); Spring and All (1923); The Great American Novel (1923); The Descent of Winter (1929); A Novelette (1932); and

The history of western art is also a history of picture frames understood as windows onto another world.

This history might begin with Leon Battista Alberti's fifteenth-century description of the picture frame as an open window through which he see what he want to paint and Leonardo da Vinci's claim that perspective is nothing else than the seeing of an object be hind a sheet of glass. By the nineteenth century, an expanded window/painting metaphor informed the development and theorization of realism such that French art critic Charles Blanc used "the window metaphor" to describe naturalism, and Emile Zola praised Monet's painting as a window open to nature. For these painters and theorists, the window was used as a heuristic device, as a metaphor that facilitated pictorial practice.By the first decades of the twentieth century, when Georges Braque challenges the window metaphor – and referentiality more generally – by painting a violin in a way no one could ever actually see it (from three different vantage points simultaneously), he is not suggesting that his painting is interchangeable with a window but that it might be possible to abstract visual representation without losing the particularity of the violin. Whereas paintings through the nineteenth century were frequently formulated as metaphorical windows onto another world, and then, by the1920s writers like Pound were implying that aesthetic frames around art literally functioned like windows, albeit negatively. Frames blocked the "flux of life" from art. (Siraganian 83)

The Observer and the Observed as Co-maker in Williams' Poetics

Marcel Duchamp's various "window" works from the teens and early 1920s, such as his masterpiece, *The Large Glass* (1915-1923) takes this idea of pictures as windows and realizes its aesthetic possibility. We know from Williams' *Autobiography* that he saw *The Large Glass* in Duchamp's studio, singling out the work as simultaneously challenging, intimidating, and inspiring. More important, "he chose to adapt Duchamp's formulations about glass windows for his own account of framing" (Siraganian 86).

Restricting individual men's actions is for Williams, finally, restricting the possibility of men's fulfilling their potential contact with the everyday world. Individual's antithesis is the organization of society which treats of men as a mass rather than as unique individuals. While he acknowledges the practical necessity for some sort regulation in men's lives, he can't accept the organization he sees, as it is primarily upon the inherently limited rational understanding. This attitude, Williams has had since the early poems, and by the time of *Al Que Quiere*, 1917, we find it fully articulated in his glass poem "Tract" (1917). The poem is a valuable statement of Williams' view of the propriety of the natural as contrasted to the impropriety of social convention, of the inherent dignity of men as opposed to the degradation of men by the shames of society. In essence, his basic requirement in the poem is that we accept reality and refuse – as he refuses – to make it look like what it is not. He begins with:

> I will teach you my townspeople
>
> how to perform a funeral –
>
> for you have it over a troop
>
> of artists –

> unless one should scour the world –
>
> you have the ground sense necessary.

Having established his belief in their innate ability to act with propriety, he instructs them.

> I begin with a design for a hearse.

But his hearse is to be neither black nor white,

> For Christ's sake not black –
>
> nor white either – and not polished!
>
> Let it be weathered – like a farm wagon –
>
> with gilt wheels (this could be
>
> applied fresh at small expense)
>
> or no wheels at all:
>
> a rough dray to drag over the ground.

In short, make things natural, let the vehicle represent its content and its function; let it show the erosion of life, with the gilt, applied specially for each use, perhaps to symbolize the wagon's specialness of purpose and the essential goodness of life. And then the afterthought: it might be most fitting to use a dray to convey the mere physical remains to their union with the other clay. From this he proceeds to advise knocking out the glass and to demand:

> Knock the glass out!
>
> My God – glass, my townspeople!
>
> For what purpose? Is it for the dead

to look out or for us to see

how well he is housed or to see

the flowers or the lack of them –

or what?

Nor may there be

Let there be no glass –

and no upholstery, phew!

and no little brass rollers

and small easy wheels on the bottom –

my townspeople what are you thinking of?

This is the crux of the poem: what is the purpose of each of the elements that Williams condemns? His implied answer is that they are meant to pervert the appearance of things and to mask reality, to gain the accommodation to ease sought in usual life. He goes on, therefore, to rule out wreaths, and especially hothouse flowers:

Some common memento is better,

something he prized and is known by:

The only natural symbol by which we should remember the man is that which truly represents him in his individuality: we must not distort his image. And finally Williams gives the instructions for the driver and the mourners: take the driver down and make him walk inconspicuously – he is only a function of the corpse. As for ourselves, we must

Walk behind – as they do in France,

seventh class, or if you ride

Hell take curtains! Go with some show

of inconvenience; sit openly –

to the weather as to grief.

Or do you think you can shut grief in?

What – from us? We who have perhaps

nothing to lose? Share with us

share with us – it will be money

in your pockets.

Go now

I think you are ready. (*CP I* 72)

It is obvious that as in so many other poems the basis here for all of Williams' objections and advice is his belief that the conventions of our society are forces for isolation, for the senseless divorce of things. As a matter of fact, "Tract" could be worked out almost perfectly as a symbolic statement of advice to the artist regarding the practice of his art. It begins by advising the artist not to be arty, or an artist before all: be a man first, an artist second. Next, in the design for the hearse, it warns against using borrowed forms and advises a rough naturalness, a form that will represent the actual world. Third, Williams says: don't use the "hothouse flowers" of "poetic" language, use the natural idiom. Then, as a continuation of the idea, he proposes avoidance of the easy but false "poetic" clichés and conventional, artificial metaphors: use true "mementoes" – actuality – as symbols. Going further, he contends that the poet as poet is unimportant and should not be discernible – the poem is what matters, nothing else. And he concludes with the advice to be open to experience and to make it available as useful knowledge.

Similarly, another Williams' early poem "Rendezvous" (1914):

> My song! It is time!
>
> Wider! Bolder! Spread the arms!
>
> Have done with finger pointing.
>
> Open windows even for the cold
>
> To come whistling in, blowing the curtains:
>
> We have looked out through glass
>
> Long enough, my song.
>
> Now, knowing the wind's knack,
>
> We can make little of daring:
>
> Has not laughter in the house corners
>
> Spoken of it – the blind horse:
>
> Has not every chink whispered
>
> How she rides biting its ears,
>
> How she drives it in secret?
>
> Therefore my song – bolder!
>
> Let in the wind! Open the windows!
>
> Embrace the companion
>
> That is whistling, waiting
>
> Impatiently to receive us! (*CP I* 36)

It reflects Williams' hostility toward the idea of constricting frames, provides a clear explanation of both his opposition to aesthetic framing and his aim for creation in his writing. Here, Williams imagines his new poetry as the long-lost contact between the poet and the wind of the world. By urging his poem to relinquish "finger pointing" – both the act of blaming others and, here, a gesture of distancing – the speaker insists on a new aim for representation because "finger pointing" implies a hostile relationship between sign and referent. In response, the speaker implores his poetic song to practice a kind of semiological calisthenics ("Wider! Bolder! Spread the arms!), forgoing representation's glass window separating the poet from the world. Williams' (like Pound's) "songs" imply a literary rebelliousness. The wind that in Coleridge's famous poem once "caress'd" his Aeolian harp is now gripped forcefully and without mediation: "Embrace the companion," writes Williams in the last stanza of "Rendezvous," "That is whistling, waiting / Impatiently to receive us!" The poem aims to render irrelevant the glass separate art from life.

"Rendezvous" describes the exciting, illicit meeting between an audience member and an art object once art frames become window frames. Before art's frame kept air and time from art, this appointment was (theoretically) impossible. But in modernity, warm song-air meets the cold air of the world of the reader, whereas art objects incorporate the sharp intake of breath from a shocked gallery observer or a reader. From Williams' perspective, observer's or reader's experiences complete the artwork.

Both of these "glass" poems imply a literary rebelliousness, and aims to render the irrelevant glass separating art from life because such an object – a medium – impedes art. Where a medium was previously understood as necessary for the very creation of an art object, here we see the medium being imagined quite differently, as an obstruction in the newly mimetic art object. The poem urges us to forget the frame and allowed in "the flux of life," and it claims Williams' poetic ambition of breaking the barrier between art and life. From Williams' perspective, readers' or observers' experience completes the artwork. By insisting upon "no ideas but in things," he forces his readers or the observers to discard their assumptions about the world, forces them to examine the object in his poems for what they are in themselves, not for what they represent. Similarly with the impressionist writers, Williams' writing provides his readers a new act of seeing.

Chapter 4

The Act of Perception in Williams' Poetry

"The most important characteristic of impressionism lies in its insistence on the perceptual reality instead of the conceptual one. The act of perception is more important than either the perceived or the perceiver" (Kronegger 67). The objects which each work contains are the successive contents of the consciousness, that of the narrator. There is no separation between the narrator and the objects: "there is a narrator seeing the objects and without objects there can be no self, and without self there can be no objects" (Kronegger 40). Positively, Williams agrees with the outlook of the impressionists that an object is important only in its relationship to the consciousness in which it has appeared. By insisting upon "no ideas but in things," Williams advocates consciousness must be consciousness of something.

4.1   A Fresh Relationship with the Everyday World

In addition to impression, the impressionists used another word to describe what they saw and painted. This was the word "sensation." Sometimes they, or their critics, used the two words almost interchangeably. In French, "sensation" is cognate with the verb *sentir* ("to feel"), and thus implies a feeling same as a perception. So, in 1870 Paul Cézanne tried to justify his recent painting by saying "I have very strong sensations" (Smith

22), as if to suggest the peculiarity of his works was owing to the fact that he painted sensations that were personal and unique to him. The impressionists have set out to develop their own originality by abandoning themselves to their personal sensations. Actually, to impressionists, the whole technical power of painting depends on our recovery of what may be called "the innocence of the eyes"; that is to say, a sort of childish perception of these flat stains of color, merely as such, without consciousness of what they signify, – as a blind man would see them when suddenly gifted with sight. In the same vein, Cézanne suggested that the painter should see like a man who has just been born (Smith 28). Raw sensations, unaffected by knowledge and experiences like touch, took the form of color patches, rather as the vision of a blind man who has just regained his sight did. Sensations, then, were supposed to be formless in the sense that they were mere visual events with no informational or cultural content – patches of color in the perceiver's mind, and no more.

At the centre of literary impressionist aesthetics is the act of perceiving the outside world and the manner in which it is perceived. The literary impressionists not only reacted against the cumbersome paraphernalia of ordinary realistic investigation, they also objected to conventional Realism because it was mechanical, clumsy and superficial, creating a merely orderly catalogue of externals, but most of all because they thought it was unreal. Several early poems of Williams are interpreted in this part to give good examples of how, more than anyone else in modern American poetry, Williams has brought attention to the things of our world, to acknowledge the everyday experience of "the flux of life." Williams has said the poem's "sensuality" is the poem's rootedness in the physical world of actuality. Only in the ordered sensuality of the poem, then, can ideas be sustained – by the constant presentness of the poem's "things." From this world the ideas may become explicit statements, rising, as it were, as the poet's imagined continuations of the structure of actuality in the poem, or they may remain unstated, implicit in the poem's order.

"To a Solitary Disciple" (1917) is a particular helpful exposition of the idea,

> Rather notice, mon cher,
>
> that the moon is
>
> tilted above
>
> the point of the steeple
>
> than that its color
>
> is shell-pink.
>
> Rather observe
>
> that it is early morning
>
> than that the sky
>
> is smooth
>
> as a turquoise.

It talks about what sort of things to use in a poem, and how to use such things, but the poem attempts to teach by doing. Here, Williams' advice is addressed to the problem of creating a poetic world of sufficient "sensual" actuality to remain always in its own here and now. He begins the poem, therefore, by making clear the foundation for all his practice: first seek out the thing itself in its uniqueness and present that. Don't talk about secondary or abstracted or commonly held qualities, although they may be more "impressive", until the poem has established what the things are and how they are ordered.

> Rather grasp
>
> how the dark

converging lines

of the steeple

meet at the pinnacle –

perceive how

its little ornament

tries to stop them –

See how it fails!

See how the converging lines

of the hexagonal spire

escape upward –

receding, dividing!

– sepals

that guard and contain

the flower!

Avoid the conventional metaphoric observations (here of color and texture) because, he implies, they are sterile; they tell us nothing we need to know. Only the direct statement of whatness contains within its sensuality – in addition to all the associational implications we can possibly want – the indispensable purely denotative knowledge of the thing as thing: the denotative fixes the poem's world in the presentness of actuality. Thus, Williams says in "To a Solitary Disciple", the restrictive fact of social convention, represented by the ornament-sign, is in opposition to the inclusiveness of the human spirit. The ornament fails to limit the converging lines because the imagination finds in them an order that it continues: this is the order of the true nature of things. In it the relationship of the human to the natural is also manifest, expressible now both by the poetic structure and by metaphor.

Observe

how motionless

the eaten moon

lies in the protecting lines.

It is true:

in the light colors

of morning

brown-stone and slate

shine orange and dark blue.

But observe

the oppressive weight

of the squat edifice!

Observe

the jasmine lightness

of the moon. (*CP I* 104)

Thus, finally, after demonstrating in the distortion of colors by the morning light how there can be a discrepancy between the real nature of a thing and our perception of it, Williams can end with a juxtaposition of images in which he can be sure his ideal will inhere. He is sure that the actuality of the poem's world will validate his judgments, which are, after all, judgments in terms of that world. The things – the edifice and the moon: the human and the natural – have been established and have their relationship and their implications. And the idea lives in them and in their order. At last Williams can use the implications of lightness and jasmineness as contradistinct from the implications of heaviness and squatness; the qualities are not, cannot be, separated from the specific, concrete objects in which they exist.

Chapter 4
The Act of Perception in Williams' Poetry

In "no ideas but in things," Williams does not mean that the poem must have no ideas; his intent is quite simply that it ought to have no ideas as pure, unattached intellect, outside the limits of what is expressed by the world of actuality. Precisely because ideas are important they must root and live in the objects or relations of objects in the poem. Whereas traditional writers and painters started from a definable subject, that is, experience previously organized and interpreted by the observing mind, impressionist artists started from perception. They rejected the traditional emphasis upon order, thought, and clearness. Through sensory experience, the impressionist opens a fresh relationship with the everyday world. Williams has insisted, in prose theory as in poetic practice, upon the necessity for drawing the poem's materials from the familiar world.

As a consequence, William's standards for beauty and goodness are different from the commonly accepted, and they are often difficult for the reader to accept, simply because the reader does not really understand them. His attitudes toward the conventions of beauty are put effectively in one of his early short poems, "Apology." (1917)

> Why do I write today?
>
> The beauty of
> the terrible faces
> of our nonentities
> stirs me to it:
>
> colored women
> day workers –
> old and experienced –
> returning home at dusk
> in cast off clothing

faces like
old Florentine oak.

Also

the set pieces
of your faces stir me –
leading citizens –
but not
in the same way. (*CP I* 70)

The beauty he sees is both real in itself and a product of his social feelings; it is the unnoticed beauty of the modern actual world as opposed to the conventionally accepted "beauty" in the illusory appearance assumed by the "set pieces." Defining good and evil acts, for the most part, in terms of expediency and usage (conventions), society's organization (government) is to his mind intrinsically pernicious. Williams has on occasion gone so far, even, as to deny the validity of the word "beauty."

But how is truth concerned in a thing so ghostlike over words as style? We may at least attempt to say what we have found untrue of it. To a style is often applied the word "beautiful"; and "Beauty is truth, truth beauty," said Keats; "that is all ye know and all ye need know." By saying this Keats showed what I take to have been a typical conviction of his time consonant with Byron's intentions toward life and Goethe's praise of Byron. But today we have reinspected that premise and rejected it by saying that if beauty is truth and since we cannot get along without truth, then beauty is a useless term and one to be dispensed with. Here is a location for our attack; we have discarded beauty; at its best it seems truth incompletely realized. Styles can no longer be described as beautiful. (*SE* 75)

What Williams has done is not, as he says, to discard beauty, but to discard the word. He has found it too encrusted with connotations of past conventional attitudes, too associated with merely a (for him) meretricious prettiness and with outworn proprieties to be useful in his world. The result of this new spirit is a beauty-in-ugliness – like the rotten apple in "Perfection" (1944, through this later work of the poet, it might be more convincible to prove that this new spirit is so deeply rooted in Williams' mind from his early time, and then as a result, it becomes quite popular in most of his artwork.):

> O lovely apple!
> Beautifully and completedly
> rotten,
> hardly a contour marred –
>
> perhaps a little
> shrivelled at the top but that
> aside perfect
> in every detail! O lovely
>
> apple! What a
> deep and suffusing brown
> mantles that
> unspoiled surface! No one
>
> has moved you
> since I placed you on the porch

rail a month ago

to ripen.

No one. No one! (*CP II* 80)

Here, even in rottenness perfection remains perfection: the color is, as Williams indicates, a beautiful deep brown, which is surely not intrinsically inferior to red or green; the surface is as smooth as it was a month before; the shape has not altered significantly and is still pleasing. Regarded as a physical entity, then, regarded as a thing seen, dissociated from the usual consideration of its food qualities, the apple is logically an excellent example of perfection. It shocks us, as it is supposed to, since Williams' intent is to break out of the conventional bound of "beauty" and to expand the realm of the beautiful, thereby producing more and better means of contact with the modern world.

4.2   The Immediacy of Impression

The literary impressionist holds that "the expression of the fleeting impression of the exterior world is more significant than the photographic presentation of cold fact" (Stowell 51). Impressionists are caught up in the transitoriness of all things. Many art critics stress the importance of this character. "Words like immediacy, transitory, fleeting, momentary, spontaneous, ephemeral, flux and Heraclitean are often used without reference to particular paintings" (Kronegger 61). Williams' writing style also aims at the great precision in the use of language to illustrate the transitory, vague, complex and subjective impressions based on experience. Two impressionist paintings are illustrated here and also several early poems of Williams' are selected in this part to demonstrate that the very important characteristic of impressionistic artwork, the immediacy of impression, is a significant character in Williams' poetry creation as well.

In their efforts to paint a scene as it appeared at the first glance, the impressionists were in fact choosing to show how it appeared in a specific and very brief time. As Shelden Cheney remarks: "Impressionism had worked realism down into the ultimate corner: where not merely any imitation of nature would do, but only an imitation of an immediate and evanescent aspect of nature" (Cheney 76).

In Renoir's *Moulin de la Galette* (1876, Figure 3), for example, placing his models under trees so that they were sprinkled with spots of light falling through the foliage, he studied the strange effects of green reflections and luminous speckles on their faces, dresses or nude bodies. His models thus became merely media for the representation of curious and momentary effects of light and shadow which partly dissolved forms and offered to the observer the gay and capricious spectacle of dancing light. The painter is concerned with the effect of spots of sunlight on skin and clothes: this required him to paint quickly before the spots of light moved or changed their angle enough to produce a different effect. (of course he chose not to paint any spots unflattering to his models.) His painting are thus identified with a specific time of day and weather condition. Edgar Degas also sought transitory effects, but more by stopping motion than by changes of light and weather. His painting of horse riding, women at their bath and his ballet dancers are good examples of this special interest. Degas refused to be identified with the impressionists, yet most art critics give him the label of being an impressionist. Indeed, he expresses some tenets of impressionist theory. In his *Les Courses de Chevaux* (1885-1888, Figure 4), for instance, the colored silhouettes of the jockeys give the impression of immediacy: at the edge of the composition, horses and people are cut across in order to induce a sense of the space and to lead us into the painting. Thus, this painting suggests the movement and not the static quality of the jockeys. There are no strong defining lines, edges, or limits.

Arnold Hauser makes an extreme statement of the transitory aspect of Impressionism:

> The dominion of the moment over permanence and continuity, the feeling that every phenomenon is a fleeting and never-to-be-repeated constellation, a wave gliding away on the river of time, the river into which one cannot step twice, is the simplest formula to which impressionism can be reduced. The whole method of impressionism is bent on giving expression to this Heraclitean outlook and on stressing that reality is not a being but a becoming, not a condition but a process. Every impressionistic picture is the deposit of a moment in the perpetuum mobile of existence, the representation of a precarious, unstable balance in the play of contending forces. (Hauser 169)

The typical impressionist subjects are landscapes, cityscapes, still lifes, and people painted as though they were still alive. What is ephemeral about a landscape or a still life? Probably this idea is suggested by the hazy effacing of contours typical of the impressionists, and also by some real effort on their part to replace the lost spiritual values of their era with fleeting sensory experience.

The impressionist painters have been struggling to capture "the moment" on their spatial canvas, in order to seize the instant in time and isolate it, transposing space into time through the vibrancy of color juxtapositions, the movement of objects in the surrounding world and the outlines of their frames. (Gunsteren 60) The language of literary impressionism is suffused with "instants", "moments", "seconds" and "minutes", creating harmony of immediacy.

After *Kora in Hell* Williams continued to experiment with the techniques he has learned from the visual arts during the years between 1913 and 1917. Many of his poems in his next book of poetry, *Sour Grapes* (1921), reflect those efforts. "The Great Figure" is perhaps one of the most effective.

> Among the rain
> and lights
> I saw the figure 5
> in gold
> on a red
> firetruck
> moving
> tense
> unheeded
> to gong clangs
> siren howls
> and wheels rumbling
> through the dark city. (*CP I* 174)

Here, the immediacy of the flashed image seen against a "dark" "rumbling" background is reminiscent of many paintings of impressionism. The urban landscape of the poem is blurred in the refracted light of a night rain, deafened by the cacophony of clangs and howls, and made to seem altogether unstable and tumultuous by its central image of tension, speed, and change, which Williams emphasizes both by placing the lines "moving / tense" at the poem's heart and by moving us in short, tension-ridden, one-world lines through that centre. Juxtaposed to this world is the figure 5 The clarity of its vision opposes itself to an almost completely confusing (and, in the context of a fire, destructive) movement, even as the brightness of its gold color on a red field opposes itself to the "dark city." If the figure is "unheeded," that is because it has so little to do with the world from which it has been lifted. The clarity, the sharpness of its focus upon the common things in our life, gives it an importance, an immediacy that force it upon our attention as it would come to our notice in the everyday life. In his *Autobiography* Williams recalls the circumstances of its genesis:

> Once on a hot July day coming back exhausted from the Post Graduate Clinic, I dropped in as I sometimes did at Marsden Hartley's studio on Fifteenth Street for a talk, a little drink maybe and to see what he was doing. As I approached his number I heard a great clatter of bells and the roar of a fire engine passing the end of the street down Ninth Avenue. I turned just in time to see a golden figure 5 on a red background flash by. The impression was so sudden and forceful that I took a piece of paper out of my pocket and wrote a short poem about it. (*Au* 172)

The image "flashes" onto the poet's field of awareness, is suspended and lifted outside the sequence of time – a snapshot taken by the poet's perception, as it were – and when the imagination takes hold of it the action has been caught and continues forever because of that. In the poem, movement is stilled within time, but continues on a new, strictly limited, plane outside of time, determined no longer by actual progression but by visual tensions. The poet now analyzes the details of his unit of perception and transposes them by means of verbal equivalents on to paper in the order of their visual importance. The poem is the painting which results, its words are the pigment. The effects of instantaneous perception and of continued movement lifted out of the usual sequence and development of time which result could not have been achieved by a prose statement or a conventional poem dependent on narrative sequence and metaphor, which would have failed to isolate the incident in its original intensity. The poem as it stands is the product of a visual experience.

Williams' determination to eliminate narrative sequence in his poetry was based on his desire to achieve the sense of visual unity and consequently, the immediacy of impression which is associated with painting. What all impressionist writers wish to achieve is harmony, a rhythmical effect beauty, stressing the autonomy of their creation. Their work reflects dominion of the passing mood over the permanent qualities of life. The sum total of these underlying forces which are evident in the ideas of the age: change, flux and instability, detachment, fragment. Scenes from the dynamic everyday world of speed and change are presented in the light of atmospheric color effects which, paradoxically, do not invite to action, but contemplation. What is broadly similar to many impressionist paintings is that they exhibit a certain degree of sketchiness. But this is not the result of incompetence or hasty working, as critics implied. Sketchiness is deliberately present in impressionism from the very beginning, in Monet's *Terrace at Sainte-Adresse* (1867, Figure 5). In this case, assuming Monet had an intention which found coherent expression in this work, it seems inevitable that he made the painting sketchy in order that it could convey something of his experience of the rapid movement in the scene depicted. It would be naïve to think that Monet achieved his all simply by working rapidly. Probably some of the initial notations were done quickly, but to achieve such spectacular results would have taken many sessions, and patient, careful reworking of the initial layers of paint. The painting might look "spontaneous," but only as the result of careful calculation.

Williams, in his early times, under the influence of impressionism, has already been writing down flashes of insight about single objects. The poems which resulted from his practice occasioned Kenneth Burke's remark, in his review of *Sour Grapes*, that "what Williams sees he sees in a flash." Many of these "flashes," however, still found their way into Williams' larger, synthetic, poems, becoming part of a simultaneous field of objects instead of being stand on their own, and this was to be the case throughout Williams' career as a poet. Still, when Burke remarked about Williams' method that "there is the eye, and there is the thing upon which that eye alights; while the relationship between the two is a poem, and defined the poet's concern with "contact" to mean "man with nothing but the thing and the feeling of that thing," he showed very clearly how close Williams had come already to the ideal of the American moment. Like impressionists Williams began to let the object speak for him by letting it speak for itself through his description of it and through the selection he made of his visual detail. Thus he learned that a poem about a single object need not necessarily be confined to two or three lines, but could, like "The Great Figure," for instance, expand according to the selection of relevant supporting detail the poet decided to include. That selection itself, however, should be representative of compressive extraction, for, as Williams now stressed, a characteristic of all good art is its compactness. It is not, at its best, the mirror – which is too ready a symbol. It is life – but transmuted to another tighter form, and restricted to essentials.

The poems in Williams' "*Spring and All*" reflect his attempts to put these ideas to practice. "The Red Wheelbarrow" (*CP I* 224) of *Spring and All* is perhaps one of the best examples. The poem is a perfect representation of the kind of painting the impressionist painters might have produced: it is a moment, caught at the point of its highest visual significance, in perfectly straightforward, but highly selective detail; each word has its intrinsic evocative function, focusing the object and its essential structural relationship to its immediate surroundings in concrete terms. The object, moreover, retains complete autonomy: it is in no way to be construed as a metaphor; rather, the very fact of its actual existence within the objective world, exactly according to the terms in which it is described, constitutes a statement about the objective world. Because the artist has focused upon the object under these particular circumstances, has seen the relationship it bears to his own position within the objective world, his statement of fact comes to represent his own feeling as well. Thus poetry, like painting, can give the inmost concerns of man a tactile reality. By focusing on an element of reality, and stripping it of all inessential detail, we can finally succeed in "raising the place we inhabit to such an imaginative level that it shall have currency in the world of the mind."[1] In the context of this visual emphasis, short comments by the poet are sometimes needed where a painting or a print, which in itself is already a visual object, needs only a sketch, or a frame, or nothing at all: Williams' comments "so much depends / upon" is the verbal equivalent to the very fact of the visual existence of a painting – which is itself a statement that much depends upon the object it portrays.

The poem "Spring and All" (1923), one of the many poems about spring with which Williams liked to open his books, and one of the best, is a landscape, much like brooding paintings in which impressionists presented elements of nature as equivalents to his innermost emotions:

> By the road to the contagious hospital
>
> under the surge of the blue
>
> mottled clouds driven from the

---

[1] Memory Script of a Talk Delivered at Briarcliff Junior College, November 29, 1945," unpublished ms. In the Lockwood Memorial Library, State University of New York at Buffalo.

> northeast – a cold wind. Beyond, the
> waste of broad, muddy fields
> brown with dried weeds, standing and fallen
>
> patches of standing water
> the scattering of tall trees
>
> All along the road the reddish
> purplish, forked, upstanding, twiggy
> stuff of bushes and small trees
> with dead, brown leaves under them
> leafless vines – (*CP I* 183)

Sketchiness of description, the poet's ability to present "outline of leaf," and a careful selection of natural detail, is the key to Williams' success here. The cloud, the dried weeds, standing and fallen, the patches of standing water, the tall tree – all are equivalents to feeling, expressive of the human condition. So are the reddish, purplish, forked bushes along the road and the dead brown leaves, the leafless vines, which constitute precisely the structure which impressionist painters constructed in so many of their paintings.

Thus we can see that Williams, the same to the impressionists, despite claiming to write spontaneously and innocently what he saw and felt (that is his impressions and sensations), paradoxically had to learn to achieve the desired effect by using some revolutionary skills.

4.3 The Conflict between Sensual Response and Rational Response

Literary impressionism opens a new way to see the world and human consciousness. That is to say, "the truth of the outside world is the impression it produces on the sensitive mind. And from that impression, man in turn knows himself" (Bender 27). Impression is the bridge connecting the world and man, the observed and the observer. In painting, the painter's impression is purely his sensation. While, in writing, impression includes sensual responses (the observers' original and pristine feelings evoked by the observed) and rational responses (the outcome of the habit and human convention) as well. Man is social. When the observed registers an impression in the observers' consciousness, it evokes both the perceptional response as well as rational one. Contrary to sensual perception which is in flux and is changing frequently, the rational response is fixed and mechanic. In the impressionistic literature, the writer strives to represent not the integrity, but the conflict of the two responses. The chief goal of literary impressionism is to represent the conflict between the two opposite responses. The poet, Williams, is also always annoyed by the two mixed feelings. Here, take the poem, "To a Solitary Disciple," (*CP I* 104) for example, in the first two stanzas of the poem he adjures his friend to choose the observations of whatness that lead one to reality, rather than those statements of similarity that present inessential aspects of actuality. In the third and fourth stanzas Williams goes beyond the simple notice of physical actuality to a more direct statement of the reality of the relationships of steeple and ornament and some of the implications that arise from their order. He returns in the following stanza to a juxtaposition of, first, an image of congruence of the two modes, the "eaten moon" lying in "the protecting lines," and, second, an image of their difference, the true colors of the slate and the stone being distorted by "the light colors / of morning." Finally, Williams is able to oppose the essential realities of the two representative objects, the "oppressive weight" of the edifice, symbolizing restrictive social organization, and the "jasmine lightness" of the moon. This is a juxtaposition and contrast that, in the light of our usual concepts of humanity and its agencies of regulation (whether secular or spiritual), certainly implies a disjuncture between what is and what we believe (because we wish it to be so).

Since Williams' main goal in his poems is not a debunking of conventional attitudes but an assertion of new values, it is necessary for him at this stage to point out didactically the importance of the seemingly banal. Ideally, Williams had already recognized at this time, things should speak for themselves (Heal 21), and he gradually developed subtler rhetorical means to achieve his aims; but even in his most didactic poems the clash between the value attributed to the depicted objects and their seeming triviality creates a tension that adds at least as much to the impact of the poems as it detracts from them.

Whereas in the earliest of these poems Williams often starts with one or several images and then, at the end, asserts their meaning, he later often anticipates it and thus creates a specific expectation:

> So much depends
> Upon
>
> a red wheel
> barrow…
>> (*CP I* 224)

or:

> I must tell you
> this young tree…
>> (*CP I* 266)

Another procedure is to start with lavish praise and then add a detail that takes us by surprise and lets us recognize that the poem deviates radically from a traditional attitude to the things depicted. Take "Perfection"(*CP II* 80) for example, together with the title, the device of invocation and the exclamation in the first line create the expectation of a poetic world with a suitably lofty style, which is then debunked in two steps: "O lovely..." clashes first with "apple." The apple itself is surely not an appropriate subject for an invocation, although it is at least familiar as a classical motif in painting. But then, as soon as we have adjusted to the level of a still life, we are confronted with an even more unexpected continuation "beautifully and completely / rotten." The poem as a whole repeats these juxtapositions in a subtler way, gradually adjusting our vision until we understand and empathize with the speaker's delight in the perfection revealed by the last stage of the cyclic process of growth and decay.

An early poem with the same device of opening invocation is "Smell!" (*CP I* 92), where the speaker seems to evoke a sublime landscape in the first line, only to deflate those expectations by the word "nose" at the beginning of the second line. (The nose is invoked here as a kind of ersatz muse, a guide to the treasures of the world around the poet):

> Oh strong-ridged and deeply hollowed
> Nose of mine! What will you not be smelling?

In his first critical essay, "America, Whiteman, and the art of poetry" (1917), Williams stressed the urgent need for an American poetry that was "free to include all temperaments, all phases of our environment, physical as well as spiritual, mental and moral. It must be truly demomcratic..."[1] Forty years later, looking back on his lifelong concern, he said in an

---

[1] "American, Whiteman and the Art of Poetry," The poetry Journal, 8:1 (Nov. 1917): 29

interview: "Anything is good material for poetry. Anything. I've said it time and time again."[1]

In the poems of *Spring and All,* a basic tension underlies the many juxtapositions and clashes, namely, the dialectics of accepting or offering resistance to the forces that make up this world. On the one hand, they are welcomed as being full of an exuberant vitality, turning the city into a place of infinite possibilities of self-fulfillment for the individual:

> Thither I would carry her
>
> among the lights –
>
> Burst it asunder
> break through to the fifty words
> necessary – *(CP I* 187)

On the other hand, the dominant forces can also appear malignant, making the city a place of mad, violent, chaotic activities, cancerous in their growth and inimical to the individual, who is always on the brink of being torn into the torrents of life – submerged, sucked up by the "dynamic mob" that fills the "swarming backstreets," stadiums, and movie houses "with the closeness and / universality of sand" *(CP I* 214). This mob is moved by its own spirit and imposes its own order; it has many faces, "beautiful" as well as "terrifying"[2], and extends from cheering crowds at ball games to the "Inquisition, the / Revolution." Again, to come to terms with these forces means to acknowledge as well as to oppose them, to face them as a life force "to be warned against // saluted and defied."[3]

The poet, too, as an paradigmatic individual, is threatened with being

---

[1] *Paterson.* Rev. ed. By Christopher MacGowan. (New York: New Directions, 1992), 222
[2] *Paterson.* Rev. ed. By Christopher MacGowan. (New York: New Directions, 1992), 233.
[3] *Paterson.* Rev. ed. By Christopher MacGowan. (New York: New Directions, 1992), 233.

overwhelmed by a mass society. There are moments when it seems utterly futile to him to set his own poems against the omnipresent language of the metropolis, the countless bits and pieces of advertising slogans, warnings, and newspaper headlines which turn the city into a gigantic college of text:

> Somebody dies every four minutes
> in New York State –
>
> To hell with you and your poetry –
> You will rot and be blown
> through the next solar system
> with the rest of the gases –
>
> What the hell do you know about it?
>
> AXIOMS
>
> Don't get killed
>
> Careful Crossing Campaign
> Cross Crossings Cautiously
>
> THE HORSES   black
>   &
> PRANCED   white (*CP I* 232)

In a world, however, in which "destruction and creation / are simultaneous," the poet realizes that this language has its own vigor and its own beauty. For the poet, as well as for the painter, the details that will be relevant can, and must, be discovered all around him, readily available to the artist who genuinely sees and hears – "It fell by chance on his car but he was ready, he was alert!" the narrator notes in *The Great American Novel.*[1]

In Williams' view, it is constantly deceiving us and constantly being glossed over by the official means of "knowledge." It is therefore dangerous, he asserts, for we form our scales of values, we ground our ideas, we judge and guide our actions, in the mistaken notion that the two are the same. Our constant attempts to attain a more nearly ideal world go away because we misunderstand both what exists and what we must do, what order we can and must give our world, if we are to achieve better lives. Williams believes we must found our actions, our lives, on the stability of truth, not on misunderstanding – on the useful knowledge of the nature of things rather than on the illusory surface of actuality. His choice is obviously a reflection of the sharp conflict between the two opposite responses in his mind.

---

[1] Imaginations, ed. Webster Schott (New York, 1970), 171.

Chapter 5

Spatial Time in Williams' Poetry

Literary impressionism suggests an emotional reality, that reality is a synthesis of sense impressions. For the impressionist,

> Space, like time, has become a surrounding atmosphere which cannot be measured or analyzed scientifically, only grasped intuitively, in a synthesis. It surrounds everything, and bounds nothing. The impressionists call spaces and times as appropriately sensations as colors and sounds. The unity of space and color sensation is for the impressionists an interplay of the individual's consciousness and the surrounding world. Reality, for the impressionist, has become a vision of space, conceived as sensations of light and color. (Kronegger 48)

Space is defined as the relationships which pieces of matter, in our experience, have with one another. Time, also is the relationship between different occasions, again within the experience of the individual's consciousness. "With the literary impressionism, the antithesis between the ego and the world, between sensation and the object vanishes. All that exist is in contact with everything else" (Gunsteren 59). Time seems to be abolished. Characters, gestures, objects and words seem to be the elements of the same atmosphere. Only characters are presented as rather static figures, in a moving atmosphere perceived at a certain distance. The self of these characters is not simply split, as with the Romantics, with the literary impressionist the character is atomized in the same way as light has dissolved the solidity of matter. Those paintings which are impressionistic often emphasize the atmospheric conditions in a certain place at a specific time. The reader is intended to "seize the impressionist works spatially in a moment of time, rather than a time sequence" (Kronegger 13). Light and its effect on the objects depicted are thus very important to the impressionist. This attitude toward visual art can be applied to poetry as well, especially to the work of those writers like Williams who are particularly interested in painting.

5.1   The Harmony of Light and Color

The impressionist painters had been struggling to capture "the moment" on their spatial canvas, in order to seize the instant in time and isolate it, transposing space into time through the vibrancy of color juxtapositions, the movement of objects in the surrounding world and the outlines of their frames. They were at pains to forget what they knew so as to achieve the "impression" in its original freshness. A peak in Monet's materialization of the ephemeral arrived at the cathedrals, *La Cathedrale de Rouen – plein soleil* (1894, Figure 6) realizing the agonizing fact that nature is changing so rapidly at each moment. Therefore, he hopes to eternalize the instant. The picture is not the representation of the gothic Rouen cathedral, but rather of the atmosphere in which it is immersed. This atmosphere suggests a living fluid. The form of the cathedral can only be inferred from the different intensities of light reflected from the surfaces which seem to be in dissolution. Thus, Monet creates a harmony of light and color. In *Femme a l'Ombrelle* (1886, Figure 7), we may find that

Monet's light-hearted approach is deceptive, as his paintings are immediate precursors of the anguished compositions of Van Gogh. Indeed, beauty is born of an ephemeral association of the lady, a parasol and light, of light with its life-giving vitality. Monet achieves the effect of great luminosity full of lyricism. However, he indirectly expresses some pessimism; without sunlight there seems to be no beauty; and beauty can only be fleeting. Van Gogh, when starting to paint in the impressionist way, often and suddenly felt the inner necessity to express his emotions in colors and light independent from the object under consideration. Especially when painting the portrait of one of his artist friends, impressionist aesthetic problems have suddenly been replaced by pre-eminently human problems. At the end of his career his art has become a means of expressing his personal feelings: the colors used in painting *L'Eglise d'Auvers* (1890, Figure 8) are expressive of his personal emotions and express the artist's inmost self. Thus, he exteriorizes his reaction to the world. The church becomes a symbol of his wretched and disordered existence: it expresses not only his disillusionment and distress, his disenchantment and incurable melancholy, but also his sense of guilt. The intensity of color, the vigorous drawing, reflects the frenzy of his own nature before he shots himself. Thus, he no longer abandons himself to the external world, as did the impressionists, but concentrates on the expression of his inner world, a world of fear and anguish. Both space and objects suddenly start to move.

Both impressionists and symbolists are preoccupied with images of light. For the symbolists, following the Platonic tradition, light is the equivalent of the highest spiritual principles, existing apart from matter, opening up a world not only beyond space and matter, but also beyond measurement. With the impressionists, light loses all such sacrosanct connotations. They do not assimilate light to the Good, the True, God, or the universal soul, but to their own soul.

Light is the soul of impressionist paintings, and the soul of impressionist literature. It is an element of style. If one calls a poem impressionistic, he is really saying that there is some mediating element through which the subject matter of the poem is presented. In impressionistic painting, the interaction of light and color are often vital to the composition. (Kronegger 43)

Likewise, in an impressionistic poem, the writer's response to a color or his own reaction to the object being examined may totally alter his poetic presentation. In such instance, the poet is using the color or his own mind permeates his entire work so that the reader feels he is once removed from the subject, experiencing it indirectly through the author's sensibilities, rather than through his own. Therefore, the quality of light in impressionist literature is a psychological as well as a narrative ambience; it envelops both writers and scenes.

Williams is also capable of producing an impressionistic poem in which light and color interplay as they often do in the paintings of Monet. "To a Solitary Disciple" from *Al Que Quiere!* is an interesting example of Williams' impressionist skill. Just like a word painter, the poet shows his reader an impressionistic scene, which emphasizes the atmospheric conditions in a certain place at a specific time. At the beginning of the poem, he adjures his readers to notice the pink light of the early morning and its effect on the steeple above the roof of the church.

> Rather notice, mon cher,
> that the moon is
> tilted above
> the point of the steeple
> than that its color
> is shell-pink

The pinkish light of dawn which becomes the base atmosphere of the poem penetrates through the whole poem. The pink color represents innocence and joy. The observer (or we say the reader) is adjured to choose the observation of whatness that leads one to reality in an innocent eye, to escape the restrictive social conventions represented by the ornament-sign and then to find the truth of nature.

> See how it fails!
>
> See how the converging lines
>
> of the hexagonal spire
>
> escape upward –
>
> receding, dividing!
>
> – sepals
>
> that guard and contain
>
> the flower!

His imaginations represented by "the converging lines" are finally out of the limitation of the ornament. The lines of the steeple force themselves beyond decoration. Protective of "the flower," they also extend to protect "the eaten moon."

The poem is depicted in terms of the poet's subjective responses to the color pink. It reflects the poet's recovery of what we may called the innocence of the eye, of a sort of childish perception of the world, merely as such, without consciousness of what restrictive social convention represented by the ornament sign, – as a blind man would see it if suddenly gifted with sight. In the six stanza, he depicts that:

> It is true:
>
> in the light colors
>
> of morning

brown-stone and slate

shine orange and dark blue" (*CP I* 105)

In this case, Williams' own reactions to the pink color act as the impressionistic filter or light through which the church is seen. The pinkish light of dawn penetrates through the whole poem. That implicates the narrator's determination of insisting on observing the order of the true nature of things in an innocent eye, believing his own judgment of the world around him and establishing a brand-new relationship with the daily life. In an impressionistic poetry, whatever we perceive is not material things, but only colors: color is not in the objects, but in the light. Therefore, what we receive from the poem is light, not the object which reflects the light. This seems to be the greatest contribution that impressionism brings to the modern art. It emphasizes the importance of color and light. In this poem, the pink light of early morning creates a pleasing and harmonious atmosphere which reflects the narrator's happiness of breaking out from the restriction and his plea of leaving the reader to his own eyes and his own imaginative devices for determining what the reality of the world is. Here, the poet is light personified, illuminating or dissolving itself. For Williams, a writer, looking at unban life, a subject already marvelously rich in poetic subject matter, the atmosphere of the city becomes a vibration of light and color.

In this poem, Williams contends that the world as we know it is often a distortion of the world as it exists objectively, independent of our understanding of it: not only is the extent of our knowledge at best incomplete, but within that partial body are illusions that we mistake for truth. For instance, if we consider normal daylight as the perfect illumination, the "brown-stone and slate" in the poem are the color we know from our knowledge which limits our perception, but the light of morning just like an innocent eye, in the fresh eyes of the pinkish light we see that the colors of the objects are "orange and dark blue." In a similar way we may consider the steeple as light personified object topped by the final ornament, or we may look beyond our conventional attitudes and consider the steeple as an expression of the human spirit that the ornament tries, but fails, to limit. Here, Williams would say, our sensual experiences report the fact of the world truthfully, but our knowledge is colored by our attitudes and opinions, which condition our understanding.

Williams' commentators have often associated his poem with Demuth's "ray-line" paintings of steeples, but these paintings follow the painter's late 1916 interest in Cézanne and impressionism. Williams has probably used the view from his own front door at 9 Ridge Road. Rutherford's First Presbyterian Church differs from the church of "To a Solitary Disciple" only in having an octagonal instead of a hexagonal spire. But the church is built of brown stone and the spire is slate, while the sprawl of the building in relation to its short spire certainly makes "squat" an appropriate description. Perhaps Williams deliberately changed the number of facets upon the spire to distance the composition from the doorstep perception.

Like so many of Williams' poems, Williams does not explain how the description of the poem will affect the contents of the poem. The author does not explain what the contents of the poem are; he does not indicate whether he is talking about one particular poem or poetry in general. He forces the reader to answer these questions for himself or else totally ignore the poem's ambiguous meaning. One point should be mentioned here. This dissertation has tried to interpret the poem "To a Solitary Disciple" from three different perspectives, just in order to prove that Williams has been influenced by series of minds of impressionism so greatly in his early time.

With the impressionist poet, the color of an object is not something which belongs to the object but, rather, a product of the ways in which sunlight, shadow, and reflected light play upon it. In traditional literature, color is a frequently used metaphor in the ordinary sense of vividness or piquancy, but when it is an impressionist literary creation, the meaning of such words as "red," "blue," "hot," and "cold" becomes an important question. Similar to feelings, color is susceptible to change, and is therefore alive. Things in the colors are alive as the poet is. The poet thinks with things not about them. Color, temperatures, etc. are sensations which have been variously defined as ways in which a consciousness is affected and also as properties of the objects themselves.

The general compositional strategy behind many of the poems of *Al Que Quiere!,* and the use they make of painterly elements, including impressionism, inform Williams' praise of his friend Maxwell Bodenheim in "MB" (1917).

> Winter has spent this snow
> out of envy, but spring is here!
> He sits at the breakfast table
> in his yellow hair
> and disdains even the sun
> walking outside
> in spangled slippers:
>
> He looks out: there is
> a glare of lights
> before a theater, –
> a sparkling lady
> passes quickly to

the seclusion of

her carriage.

Presently

under the dirty, wavy heaven

of a borrowed room he will make

reinhaled tobacco smoke

his clouds and try them

against the sky's limits! (*CP I* 72)

Sitting down to write, "MB" with his yellow hair produces his own light, "and disdains even the sun." Looking out at impressionistic arrangement of light, and turning into feminine expression, he prepares to compose. The quality of light here is a psychological as well as a narrative ambience: it envelops both protagonist and scene. This light never dramatizes action, but lends it calm. We wish to explore the poet's imagery of light as it calls forth a mutation of both the scene and the protagonist, and creates a new concept of allusive space. In this poem, the light washes, cleans and clarifies everything. It prepares a clear and harmonious psychological environment for MB to calm down from the irritation of many kinds of artistic conventions which limit the artist's imagination and begin his artistic composition in the newly coming day. And the composition is within his own terms – the room borrowed for the one – as he strives to become the sun within the clouds of his own tobacco smoke. "MB" moves from notice of external nature ("the snow") to perceived artistic relationship that bears an oblique relationship to the gestation occurring within the poet ("a glare of lights / before a theater") and finally to re-expression of this arrangement in personal terms with forms of the artist's own choosing. It is through light and color that the poem attempts to rise above physical limitations. The poet seeks light, and projects onto it echoes of his individual being, and he is able to make light the language of his innermost nature.

Williams' contacts with the New York avant-garde increased considerably in the years between *The Tempers* (1913) and *Al Que Quiere!* (1917). Avant-garde activity in New York, like that in London and Paris, was centered on the new developments in the visual arts. Before publication of *Al Que Quiere!* Williams had entertained the notion of subtitling the book "The pleasure of Democracy." The November 1915 *Others* carried the comment by J. B. Kerfoot on the magazine that, "It is the expression of democracy of feeling rebelling against an aristocracy of form." The sentence sums up Williams' intention. The volume was to be American expression rebelling against the conventions of European tradition, and contemporary expression rebelling against conventions suited to past eras. But the Spanish title, which means "To Him Who Wants It," emphasizes that the poems are suitable only for a limited readership. As Pound and many others had stressed, modernist art was essentially "undemocratic" in its refusal to compromise to gain an audience. Williams tried to root in the creative patterning of his own experience, and not in pre-existing conventions. By presenting the impressionistic skills as well as other revolutionary skills in poem, just the same as the "MB," in his poetry, Williams gradually built up his own set of conventions of composition.

Williams, in his early time, looked to impressionism for new strategies to bring to his poetry, and the color-light strategy becomes a very popular feature of his work. William's later work also reveals the obvious influence from impressionism. We may find that impressionistic techniques are not only applied in his early poems but also involved in his later ones. Here, the dissertation attempts to set an example to show that impressionism actually becomes an universal character of all his works. In "Choral: the

Pink Church," (1949) Williams boldly states his intention to use color and light as the bases for his examination of madness and joy by writing

> sing!
> transparent to the light
> through which the light
> shines, through the stone,
> until
> the stone-light glows,
> pink jade
> – that is the light and is
> a stone
>
> and is a church – if the image
> hold...

Williams equates the pinkness of the church with the color of a virgin's nipples and eventually with the innocence of joy and divine madness.

The color pink and the pinkish light of dawn permeate the entire poem. After stanza three, the innocence of the pink church which trembles in the dawn is replaced by the wildness of "drunks, prostitutes, Surrealists – ...Poe, Whiteman, Baudelaire" and the importance of

> the – banded-together
> in the name of
> the Philosophy Dep'ts
> wondering at the nature
> of the stuff
> poured into
> the urinals
>   of custom...

Above these ineffective philosophers and their greater colleagues, John Dewey and William James, stands

> the Pink Church:
>
> the nipples of
>
> a woman who never
>
> bore a
>
> child... (*CP II* 177-180)

The church, the virginal nipples, and the woman herself represent that kind of innocent knowledge which can not be equaled by even the most erudite minds. Yet, at the same time, "the fool / the mentally deranged / the suicide / sucked of its pink delight." Williams, or the narrator of his poem, seem to be saying here that knowledge and madness are nurtured by the same source which is represented by the pink church. In the final portion of this chorale, the narrator tells all men to respond to the knowledge of joy which may sometimes be akin to madness or at least to the agony endured by Samson after Delilah's betrayal. Here again the implication is that madness and joy may have similar inspirations.

In the final line of his poem, Williams describes John Milton, the author of *Samson Agonietes*, as a communist. Communism has commonly been associated with the color red and so in this final word, Williams has moved from the innocent pinkness of the church toward the redness of communism. Red is a bright, sometimes harsh, color and seems an appropriate hue for the ending of a poem which has dealt in large part with madness and ignorance.

In noting Williams' impressionistic use of color in "Choral: the Pink Church," one is only barely touching the significance of the poem. It is true, though, that the color pink is juxtapose against the harsh and ugly realities of drunks and ignorant fools. It is the diffusion of this color throughout the poem and its symbolic value as a representation of innocence and joy which make the rest of the poem's content more bearable to the reader. Indeed, the importance of the poem seems to change with each rereading, in much the same way that color emanating from a prism varies as the prism is moved. Williams is a successful poet. His willingness to experiment with various literary forms is a proof to his adventurous spirit.

5.2　The Philosophy of Water

It seems that both impressionist painters and writers are always more attracted by water than by people. Water is a very important philosophic image of impressionism. Essentially, the theme of water is a variation of the theme of light, as water is fit to convey the meaning of light. Water sparkles in the sunshine, and the harmonious movement of water can reflect the transient effect of light and color perfectly. A river is for the painter animated surface of many colors. The river's intensity of tones, the reflection of color values are favorite studies of impressionist painters and writers.

Throughout Monet's painting career, one of his main concerns was capturing the fleeting effect of light on water. In his *On the Seine at Bennecourt* (1868, Figure 9), the woman sitting by the river is Monet's future wife, Camille, but the picture is in no way a portrait of her: Monet's interest lies not in details, but in capturing the effect of the whole scene as it would be perceived in a fleeting glance. The impermanent reflections on the river's surface appear as substantial as any of the tangible elements of the painting. Monet is an artist whose work most unequivocally represents the aims of impressionism. He was dedicated to painting in the open air, to capturing what he called the most fugitive effect of nature, and he used pure, bright colors based on what his eyes saw rather than on what the conventions of painting decreed. Abandoning traditional historical or religious themes, he also rejected the highly finished techniques of academic art. *Bathers at La Grenouillere* (1869, Figure 10) is one of the earliest examples of the new style: Monet creates a vivid impression of the bustling activity at La Grenouillere and the glittering effect of sunlight on water. The study of water played an important role in the development of the style of Monet and his friends. In 1868 Monet painted *On the Seine at Bennecourt*, the picture of a woman seated on a river bank in which the reflections on the water became one of the main features. Just as snow scenes had permitted the artist to investigate the problem of shadows, the rendering of water offered an excellent opportunity to observe reverberations and reflections. Thus they could further develop their knowledge of the fact that so-called local color was actually a pure convention that every object presents to the eye a scheme of colors deriving from its proper hue, from its surroundings, and from atmospheric conditions.

Water carries not only the brightness of light but also the implication of light. Time passes away like flowing water, water has been another way of expressing time in literature long ago. In literature the water image is used less to sing the harmony of light and color than to be the basic connection between an initial emotional state and a final emotional state, controlling the protagonist as to his wishes and feelings. In an impressionist's artificial creation, the consciousness of himself is always moved along with the movement of light and water. In the river of time he feels the stream of consciousness. Actually, the philosophy of water in impressionism is a kind of expression of stream of consciousness. Since both stream of consciousness and impressionism are expressions of time, we may find that actually the philosophy of water is the philosophy of time Time is something that we can not see or touch but can only feel its passing by. Time can be regarded as an extension of man's consciousness. Man's consciousness is so closely related to time that it can break through the confinements of time and space, set up a new world in which it can move freely, and eventually achieve the exchange of the past, the present and the future. To the impressionists, psychological time is the real time.

Stream of consciousness writing has an important but confusing relation with impressionist. Stream of consciousness writing, like impressionism, attempts to show how the external world impinges upon an individual mind. Impressionism is then one technique of stream of consciousness writing, but stream of consciousness writing is not necessarily impressionistic. Impressionism follows sensations only to the nerve-end, while stream of consciousness writing follows them into the brain to see how they disturb the stream of thought and feeling. As Ortega y Gasset says: "Not halting even at the cornea the point of view crosses the last frontier and penetrates into vision itself, into the subject himself" (Ortega 114).[1]

As Leon Edel, among others, has suggested, stream of consciousness is the logical extension of impressionistic modes of narration (Nagel 77). The process of recording sensational responses gives way rendering mental activity. Daniel G. Hoffman acknowledges Stephen Crane as a pioneer in the use of stream of consciousness. Benjamin D. Giorgio, writing in his dissertation, "Stephen Crane: American impressionist," comments more extensively:

> Although Crane's greatest achievements are in those means
> by which he rendered the "spectacle of the affair" – striking use

---

[1] The closest parallel to stream of consciousness writing in paint would be not Impressionism but those surrealistic works (such as Chagall's *I and my Village* of 1911) which combine such images and emotional colorations as might be found in a single mind. This is the last stage, says Ortega, of the disturbingly simple progression he finds from Giotto to modern painters: "First thing are painted; then, sensations; finally, ideas." (Ortega 117) These three stages correspond to the literary terms realism, impressionism, symbolism.

of color, flashing imagery, cinema-like shifting of the points of
perception, etc. – he also took significant steps toward impressionism.
Crane not only effectively conveys his characters' thoughts and
feeling through narrative means and impressionist techniques, but
he also displays an acute knowledge of the process of mental flow.
(Nagel 77)

It is not difficult to provide examples from Williams' poetry of the
kind of internal impressionism Giorgio describes. Take one of his early
poems "The Sea" from *Spring and All* (1923) for example:

> The sea that encloses her young body
> ula lu la lu
> is the sea of many arms –
>
> The blazing secrecy of noon is undone
> and and and
> the broken sand is the sound of love –
>
> The flesh is firm that turns in the sea
> O la la O
> the sea that is cold with dead men's tears –
>
> Deeply the wooing that penetrated
> to the edge of the sea
> returns in the plash of the waves –
>
> a wink over the shoulder
> large as the ocean –
> with wave following wave to the edge
>
> Oom barroom

In this poem, the style of the narration is characterized by a flow of thoughts and images, such as, the cold sea, a young woman's firm body, the dead man's tears, the broken sand, the field over there, etc., which may not appear to have a coherent structure, actually all have internal relations to each other.

> It is the cold of the sea
>
> broken upon the sand by the force
>
> of the moon –
>
> In the sea the young flesh playing
>
> floats with the cries of far off men
>
> who rise in the sea
>
> with green arms
>
> to homage again the fields over there
>
> where the night is deep –
>
> la lu la lu
>
> but lips too few
>
> assume the new – marruu
>
> Underneath the sea where it is dark
>
> there is no edge
>
> so two – (*CP I* 222)

To the poet, the cold sea represents the past, the tradition rules, which "enclose her young body". "Many arms" of the sea are trying to fasten "her young body" tightly. But "the flesh is firm that turns in the sea", she insists to struggle with "the cold sea", and tries not to be buried in "dead men's tears," since the wild sea is not her home. Escaping away from the deep seduction of the sea, she finally chooses to go to "the field over there." Here, "the field" represents the present, "the new – marruu", the root of life. The mind of the poet weaves in and out of time and space, carrying the reader through the present lifespan(or thought) of one person to incorporate the lives(or thoughts of persons from other time period). It is easy to find that the young body actually hints at every modern man with no identity. Her hesitation between the sea and the inland actually is a metaphor for all necessary processes of spiritual confusions of all modern persons.

The point of relationship between the young woman and the natural realm that makes the poem more than merely a descriptive set-piece is, of course, the statement about time. With the indirect statement about time, a new perception appears: by the motion of the young body we recognize the similar meaningful motion of the cold waves of the water; the difficulty of progress for each parallels the other and parallels also the young body's constantly difficult search for love in "the cold of the sea." The water (one of Williams' favorite poetic objects) thereby supports both the natural world and the human world. In so doing it assumes the character of time. But time is a purely human concept, and the mention of it suggests the relatedness of what is seen to the human world that sees it. Thus, the water also hints at the unity between the human world and the natural world. In many of his poems, Williams associates the water of sea or river both with the flowing of time and with language, the means of continuity and traffic among men. The river animates the city and the man, and connects each with its origins and the reality of its nature.

The use of steam of consciousness technique as a medium in Williams' poetry creates an unseen bridge composed of the thoughts and feelings of the narrators in his poems. In William's another early poem "Rain" (1930), the medium also establishes an emotional connection between the visible and invisible worlds by allowing the reader into the mind of the narrator of the poem. Let's first see the first several stanzas of this long poem:

> As the rain falls
> so does
> your love
>
> bathe every
> open
> object of the world –
>
> In houses
> the priceless dry
> rooms
> of illicit love
> where we live
> hear the wash of the
> rain –
>
> There
> paintings
> and fine
> metalware
> woven stuffs –
> all the whorishness
> of our
> delight
> sees
> from its window

At first sight of the poem, the structure of the long poem looks like the movement of the narrator's consciousness, as well as the trickles of the rain. That makes the whole poem looks like an interesting world painting.

> The trees
>
> are become
>
> beasts fresh-risen
>
> from the sea –
>
> water
>
> Trickles
>
> from the crevices of
>
> their hides –
>
> So my life is spent
>
>   to keep out love
>
> with which
>
> she rains upon
>
>   the world

Moreover, from it, we can also find Williams places more importance on capturing life in its basic, raw form, which often includes interruption from the outside world. "Your love bathe every open object of the world". Inside the window, it is "the priceless dry rooms", while outside the window, "my life is spent to keep out love with which she rains upon the world."

> the rain
>
> of her thoughts over
>
> the ocean
>
> every

where

walking with
invisible swift feet
over

the helpless
waves –

Unworldly love
that has no hope
of the world

and that
cannot change the world
to its delight –

The rain
falls upon the earth
and grass and flowers
come
perfectly

into form from its
liquid
clearness (*CP I* 343)

The rain which represents the modern ideas is "walking with invisible swift feet over the helpless waves" of the ocean, and finally the rain "falls upon the earth and grass and flowers come perfectly." The modern American people, just as the rain in this poem, after a long and hard spiritual journey finally find their identity, their spiritual home, which is not in the far wild sea but is deeply rooted in the earth, in the everyday life. Williams' goal is not to depict a "pure" idea vision of the world, but, instead, to bring elements of everyday life into his writing which will evoke familiarity between the reader and the text. For Williams, truth involves showing things in their natural state…flaws included. There is also an attempt to infuse the canvas with enough abstraction and blurred images to leave some interpretation up to the audience and their own individual experiences and responses to the poem.

To sustain the whole impression of universally difficult progress, the structure of the poem is such that movement of the rain is arduous; the statements and even words are split and carried through line ends and ends of stanzas, so that in the necessity of often reading several lines to get the whole image or idea, the movement of the poem is slow and by direct from one thing to the next, centripetal, toward unity. Just as the association of the sea with time in "The Sea" is not in itself a new or unusual idea, the identification of the water with the human mind in this poem is a familiar poetic device. "Rain" also uses the water as its means of unification between the human and the natural world. In this poem Williams establishes the point of relationship immediately, but what appears at first to be a conventional form of metaphor develops into something unusual. By the qualifications of "the rain / of her thought over / the ocean," the rain maintains its objective existence outside the mind as well as its assumed image-life within. In fact, it becomes, finally, a literal statement of what happens: that at times a man may imaginatively project himself into the world about him and identify himself with it – not as a poetic metaphor, but as psychological fact. The thought can become the center of the poem from which to view the things external to it, and at the same time it can use its very consciousness of self to establish the identity between self and them.

Thus instead of the thought being described in terms of the rain, actually the rain and its surroundings are anthropomorphized, the ocean, the earth and grass and flowers, the rain itself all becoming a replica of the thought as it sees itself and its enveloping physical features. In this way, Williams accomplishes the ambivalence that he believes is the basis of the "imaginative array" – the revelation of the quality-in-common within the uniqueness of each thing.

Writers of literary impressionism focus on emotional and psychological processes which are evolving in the minds of one or more narrators in a poem. The stream of consciousness technique takes the concept of the omniscient narrator to a new level by representing not only the internal thoughts of the main narrator, but by also acknowledging the internal observations of those who come in various levels of contact with the main narrator. Williams attempts to use the technique in his writing as a vehicle to bring her reader along for the journey into the internal world of his narrators. A further study of Williams' narration will be made in details in the next chapter (Chapter 5).

5.3   The Image of Spatial Time

The qualities of images used by the writer, of color used by the painter seem to shade off into each other. "In all impressionist creations, image and color are inseparable and interdependent" (Kronegger 80). For the impressionists, harmony is created to unite light and image, harmony is the basis of color, depending on the reflection of light on the image to be presented. Color and light provide the essential structure of the impressionist painting and literature: their unity is no longer created by linear contours but by color and light only.

It seems "the impressionist writer's recording of the sensations of light is associated with the experience of distance, and remoteness" (Stowell 239). In many of Williams' poems, images of haze, damp air, fog, mist, and smoke predominate and convey the impression of distant vision through unity of color under specific light. The writer often "hears and sees from distance only, being barely able to do either, then, is reduced to guessing and interpreting gestures and attitudes" (Stowell 237).

Impressionist paintings usually have haze contours and blurred of nonexistent details. Indeed, it was just this lack of solid form, these vaporized outlines, that Cézanne reacted against. Sometimes this blurring is a result of the atmospheric conditions in the scene rendered. For example, in Monet's *Norwegian landscape in Winter* (1895, Figure 11), the effect of observing through a heavy snowstorm is shown. He left the architectural details as blurred as the fading light rendered them. But more typically there is no apparent reason, either in the subject or the air or light conditions, why impressionists usually blurred contours and details.

Monet's *Sunflowers* (1881, Figure 12) illustrates the problem: the subject is a white vase of sunflowers and their leaves on a red tablecloth, seen in bright sunlight at a distance of about four feet. Contours and details are blurred as though seen through a thick mist or a sheet of wavy glass. The flowers themselves seem to have dissolved into areas of yellow with brown centers. Why did Monet choose not to paint details which must have been clearly visible? Since the effect is as though something is between us and the flowers, critics often speak of "atmospheric" painting, of the air itself made visible and shimmering. But the actual air in a scene is never visible, no matter how brightly lighted; one can see the atmosphere only if it contains rain, snow, fog, mist or dust, or if one looks through miles of air at distant objects.

Impressionist paintings usually have haze contours and blurred of nonexistent details, although the subjects are always easily recognized. The simplest literary analogue of this characteristic is vague, incomplete description. Williams is good at this approach in his poetry. The second version of "The Locust Tree in Flower" (1933) can be called a good example of literary impressionism. Let's see the first version firstly:

Among
the leaves
bright

green
of wrist-thick
tree

and old
stiff broken
branch

ferncool
swaying
loosely strung –

come May
again
white blossom

clusters
hide
to spill

their sweets
almost
unnoticed

down

and quickly

fall (*CP I* 366)

Then, let's see the second version of the poem. Here, in the second version, all the details of a recognizable scene lose their precision, just like Monet's *Sunflower.*

Among

of

green

stiff

old

bright

broken

branch

come

white

sweet

May

again (*CP I* 366)

Monet blurs details because he wants to render primarily the arrangement of colors; Williams subdues details and mutes sensations in order to build a mood, to suggest subtle meanings in the manner of impressionism. The technique which attempts to construct poems out of pieces of actuality is that it works always toward vagueness, toward the stripping away of all words but the absolutely indispensable denotations of the objects; it relies less than conventional verse upon particles, intensifiers, qualifiers, all the words that regulate the shades of meaning by talking about the objects. If this leads, perhaps, to less subtlety in expression of intellectual materials, it does certainly lead to great energy being pent up in the poem. The two versions of the poem exemplify how the stripping achieves such energy. Williams almost achieves what his work is always moving toward: the ultimate compression in which everything – every word, every sound, almost – is so fertile with implication that it must burst from the confines of strictest meanings and lose the half-hidden-half-felt threads of a radiating web of associations and extended meanings. Williams' contribution here is the reduction of the line to the single word. The (for Williams, at least) conventional units of structure, the line and the word, being identical, but the reader expecting more from the line than he gets, the unit leaves a vacuum, intellectual as well as emotional, that the reader must fill from the associations, the connotations, that inevitably a poem frees but too often the reader forces back into the darkness of the mind. The differences between the earlier and later versions and between one's reactions to them are evident.

To be analogous to impressionist painting, a writer would neglect details in order to record the main aspects of a scene – those parts which he immediately notices. These are normally the most conspicuous, rather than the most subtle. For example, the second version of the poem, Williams notes the green, the old bright broken branch, the white sweet May of the scene rather than inconspicuous details. Though more obviously in the second version, both of these depend to a great extent upon the convention of the line containing more than one word and more than one accented syllable – except, of course, in the cases of lines deliberately shortened for emphasis by their differences from the rest of the poem. As a result of the reader's conditioning he tends to expect more than he gets, and he is forced to seek out the implied ramifications – both logical (denotative) and associational (connotative) – of the framework – in effect to flesh out the skeleton. But there is also here the feeling of the material working to break the restrictions of the form – as there should be in any poem. The conflict between this expansive tendency of words and the restrictive nature of the poem's structure, here in the maximum possible opposition, creates the underlying energy and excitement that is the initial emotional charge in the poem.

In the second version, the impressionistic vague, incomplete description is marvelously effective. Upon first reading the poem, one is inclined to suppose that it is composed of almost nothing but nouns and verbs, of solidities and action; yet only two words are nouns – and one of them the name of a month – just one a verb. The impression of solidity, of things, derives from the isolation of words ordinarily hidden in the welter of a sentence. Finding the word "Among" immediately unrelated syntactically to anything but "of" – which makes no sense logically – the reader is forced to hold in his mind the general meaning of the word while he goes on in the poem. But "among" implies plurality, usually of concrete objects, so that one must assume the poem's field filled with things. From this idea of the distributive, one moves to the idea of the collective, the possessive, a sort of identification, in the second unit, "of." Thus if the two words do not make logical sense, they certainly make an impressionistic sort of poetic sense, especially because one must give his mind to pure concept, relationships left blank, to be filled in further on. "Green" in the next line completes the first three-line sense-unit with another dissociated quality; while conceivably the word might be used as a simple conventional modifier, it takes on a half-life of its own here, implying some possessor(s) of greenness. But "green" supplies the objective reference for the first two lines, and one finally fills out the double image of being within the green to the extent of becoming – or feeling – identified with it.

The second three-line sense-unit is built in exactly the same fashion as the first, except that the reference for the adjectives is withheld. That is, each line implies a possessor of its quality, lacking the name of that possessor, one holds the idea of physical things concurrently with the idea of stiffness, oldness, and brightness.

The third sense-unit is the pivot. The reader's mind here works in two directions at once; toward the concrete, the specific, the restricted – the branch; and toward the abstract, the general, the inclusive – the world, which the branch comes to represent. This device constantly reminds us of Poe and Joyce's world, a world constituted by the power of words, where the world of appearance is broken up into fragments. Their protagonists discover a certain significance in cracks, fissures, broken objects, ragged mountains, just like the "broken branch" in this poem of Williams. The appearance of these images of a broken world suggests that thing falls apart, that the center does not hold, and still there is an undefinable harmony created by the rhythmical effects of light and color.

In beginning with "white" the fourth sense-unit offers a possible subject, if one takes whiteness as the same sort of generalized solidity that "green" was. By considering this possibility, the reader magnifies the term, and while he later realized that the specific reference of the world is to flowers – just as the green is the leaves – he makes the quality equivalent to the thing and interchangeable with it, which is precisely what the poem has done in his own mind. The poem thus fills out all its lacunae and forms a whole image of wholeness, of the interconnectedness of leaf, branch, flower, color, smell, time. Even without the last word it would stand of its own solidity. But the last line qualifies the entire structure by its implication of evanescence, of all these elements having once been fused, then separated, as they will be again. It adds, in other words, another kind of unity, the oneness of past, present, and future.

There is one further aspect of the poem's structure that ought to be remarked – its appearance on the page. For the starkness of the poem is a reflection of the bareness of tree; at the same time, the words' pregnancy with implication and their effect of beauty are the equivalent of the beauty and promise of the flowers. Carried within the stripped poem are the same possibilities as those carried within the stripped tree. Perhaps the poem and the tree, too, become finally interchangeable.

Here, in "The Locust Tree in Flower", the objects are known as the manifestations of their selected qualities. Yet the very qualities that create the men's uniqueness, their distinctive attraction for the poet, are what make them in effect the representatives of all that is best in the world – its purity and its vitality. The poem works because it only presents the pieces until the reader has established in his own mind the point of connection that the final formal simile only reinforces.

The hazy effect is in fact a result of the basic idea of impressionism: what one sees in a first impression is not details or sharp contours, but rather the color masses in their relationship to each other. It takes a second look and some study to notice details. In addition, rapid work is required to render a scene before the elements of it change. Fast painting must necessarily skip over details. In recording a first impression of typical colorful impressionist subjects, patches of color are more important to a speedy rendering than anything else. During Monet's truly impressionist period (up to about 1890), whenever he had recorded the striking color arrangement of his subject, he stopped; nothing more was important to his particular style of painting. William's Works is often the product of the

impressionistic painter's eyes. For instance, "The Pot of Flowers" from
Spring and All (1923):

> Pink confused with white
> flowers and flowers reversed
> take and spill the shaded flame
> darting it back
> into the lamp's horn
>
> petals aslant darkened with mauve
>
> red where in whorls
> petal lays its glow upon petal
> round flamegreen throats
>
> petals radiant with transpiercing light
> contending
> > above
>
> the leaves
> reaching up their modest green
> from the pot's rim
>
> and there, wholly dark, the pot
> gay with rough moss.   (*CP I* 184)

Beginning with the topmost portion of the object he views – the part
most immediate to the viewer's notice – Williams works downward to the
plant's base in the pot; he builds from the bright colors to the dark, from
the confusion of petalled brilliance to the relative simplicity of the moss.
Word counts probably prove nothing ordinarily, but it is nonetheless
interesting to note that of the sixty-seven words in the poem twelve are

either the names of colors or descriptions of light, and ten more are the names of things that possess color or give light; one third of the poem, in short, is the presentation of light and color. The poem's effect upon the reader is therefore one of the movement of color-masses; from the beginning in the first line's mixing of pink and white as abstracted qualities, the poem moves in different vague images that each offers a different, fragmented view of the interplay between colors and between the light's true source and its seeming regeneration in the flowers' brilliance, until the unmoving "modest green" and the pot's indeterminate darkness hold the centrum of the structure.

A number of other poems from *Spring and All* would serve similar analyses. Nor is *Spring and All* the only source for evidence; Williams' deservedly praised clarity of detail, his sense of the thing as thing in all its distinctness, are constant evidence of his poems' kinship to impressionistic painting.

Chapter 6

Impressionist Narrative in Williams' Poetry

The narrating way a writer uses to present the text largely represents his (or her) way of dealing with reality and truth. Different from the traditional omniscient narrative in which the author's view dominates the way of telling, the impressionist text tries to represent the "immediate epistemological experience" (Peters 24), they advocate to render rather than narrate life.

> The true rendering of sensory experience (or one's perception), requires rigorous and austere methods, and getting rid of elements which are not fundamentally sensational". For Literary impressionists, the traditional omniscient narrative must be dismissed, since it implies assumptions about the nature of truth which are invalid. These assumptions often record not what it sees but what is perceived by a single person. The effect is a distancing, an objectivity. (Nagel 37)

Therefore, new method of narration conducive to the expression of reader's individual experiences (or perceptions) must be employed. Ford Madox Ford emphasizes that literary impression must render impressions in their work. Stephen Crane claims, "You must render, never report."[1] According to literary impressionists, limited narrative and fragmental narrative are important new narrative methods to achieve the impressionist effect.

6.1 Williams' Limited Narrative

If the central proposition of Impressionism is the literary rendering of sensory experience, the qualifying variable is the mind that perceives the sensations. This problem did not affect impressionistic painting because there was no presumed creation of human consciousness, only of the scene being perceived: the assumption is that what is depicted is rendered as what the painter saw in open air. Similarly, in music, the general assumption is that the impressions evoked through tones are those of the composer. But this assumption is not present in literary works because of the interjection of an intermediary center of intelligence which functions as narrator and which often records not what it sees but what is perceived by one of the characters. The effect is distancing, an objectivity, which makes more difficult the illusion of sensory activity. "The limitation of narrative data to the narrator's projection of the mind is essential to the concept of impressionism since it ultimately reveals that reality is not fully comprehended by a single human mentality"(Nagel 36). Views of reality in literary impressionism are therefore dependent upon the perceiving mind (or minds). It follows that the accuracy of the rendering mind often depends on the quality of the observer and the limitations his immediate position may place upon him.

---

[1] Stephen Crane, as quoted by Ford Madox Ford, "Techniques," *South Review* I . I (July 1935): 31.

James Nagel says:

> The war-correspondent arises, then, to become a sort of
> cheap telescope for the people at home: further still, there have
> been fights where the eyes of a solitary man were the eyes of the
> world; one spectator whose business it was to transfer, according
> to his ability, his visual impressions to other minds. (Nagel 37)

The awareness that what the viewer transmits is his visual impressions
of the scene is a central proposition in impressionistic aesthetics, one easily
extended from a war correspondent to the narrator.

Narrative techniques involve point of view which is empirically
verifiable and operationally (almost) concrete – is the element of structural
choice which, by itself, seems likely to make the greatest contribution to
the impressionist style. The concept of "point of view" was first introduced
into literary criticism by Percy Lubbock in his 1921 study of fiction as a
technical craft. Lubbock said:

> The whole intricate question of method, in the craft of
> fiction I take to be governed by the question of the point of
> view – the question of the relation in which the narrator stands to
> the story. He tells it as he sees it, in the first place; the reader
> faces the storyteller and listens, and the story may be told so
> vivaciously that the presence of the minstrel is forgotten…
> (Lubbock 251)

The significance of this statement is rooted in a few very basic
assumptions as to what constitutes good or effective choices as opposed to
bad or ineffective ones. This becomes a matter of the author's manipulation
or control of the "intelligence which determines the range and quality of

the scene and the action."[1]

Point of view is by no means new to fiction, but certain modes of the dramatized point of view definitely are new to all twentieth-century literature. Again as Lubbock has said:

> The spectator, the listener, the reader, is now himself to be placed at the angle of vision; not an account or a report, more or less convincing, is to be offered him, but a direct sight of the matter itself, while it is passing. Nobody expounds or explains; the story is enacted by its look and behavior at particular moments... (Lubbock 252-253)

The point of view appears to omit the author entirely. The author's focus will then become fixed so tightly to the conscious processes of the characters that the reader will not be able to distinguish between "witnessing" and "participating." It is by now generally acknowledged that the narrator's presence in or absence from a text has a crucial effect on a literary structure. The narrator is therefore the most central concept in the analysis of a narrative text. (Gunsteren 100) The identity of the narrator, his participation, his perceptibility, and the choices that are implied, all give the text its specific character.

The technical antithesis of first-person narration, with its inherent limitations, is omniscience, which has an omniscient narrator, with access to all information, free from temporal and spatial restrictions. Omniscient narration usually adopted by the traditional writers, who narrate from the comprehensive and absolute perspective, is denied by Ford Madox Ford, Stephen Crane, and other scholars. For Ford literary impressionist must render impressions in their texts. "We saw that life did not narrate, but

---

[1] Tate, Allen. "Techniques of Fiction," *Collected Essays*. Denver: Alan Swallow, 1959, 131.

made impressions on our brains. We in turn, if we wished to produce on you an effect of life, must not narrate but render impressions." (Ford 194-195)

Instead of narrating and commenting, a good impressionist writer should identify himself with the character. He confines himself to what the character experiences, feels and thinks. His narration is limited. Briefly put, the narration is restricted to what the character experiences at the very moment and the narrator pretends to know not more than what the character perceives. Impressionism breaks up the author-reader relation. Since there is no reliable narrator, the reader is forced to find the meaning of the writing and obtain the truth himself.

Literary impressionists resort to limited perspectives of different point of views to transcribe the individual perceptions of object in the world, rendering the impression of the scenes, the events they see. They, therefore, employ different methods in dealing with point of views in a manner suggesting a limitation of perception in shifting, uncertain point of view. Thus, information from multiple perspectives of different individuals was rendered. Multiple perspectives (multiple voices) play an important role in rendering the different impressions of scenes and events in impressionist literature.

In *Spring and All* and in his prologue to *Kora in Hell*, Williams demonstrates his narrative innovations, which shared with impressionism an urgent revolt against the past. Like impressionists, Williams defines tradition largely in terms of conventional or habitual ways of describing what is real. In *Spring and All,* he explains how tradition indicates to contemporary writers, robbing them of their own voice: the artist must free himself from "demoded" words and conventional associations "because meanings have lost through laziness or changes in the form of existence which have let words empty."[1] "Nothing is good save the new," Williams argued in his prologue to *Kora in Hell*, and *in Spring and All* he imagines a comic apocalypse in which all forms of representation are destroyed so that artists may recreate the world anew. The following poems of Williams are selected here to demonstrate Williams' experiment in limited narration, the multiple voices.

Williams' first efforts to write poetry with multiple voices began with "March" (1916) and "January Morning" (1917). In these two poems, Williams experimented with polyphony tentatively, as if he still depended upon the dramatic monologue that he has used for so many of the poems he has assembled for publication in *Al Que Quere!* 1917. But with "Overture to a Dance of Locomotives" (1917), Williams confidently concluded the poem by having the voices of people in a train station (in Williams' case, the newly opened Penn Station in New York City) interrupt the meditations of the poem's speaker.

In "January Morning", Williams' use of many voices is restrained, a matter of changes of inflection rather than of obviously different characters; the poem remains essentially a dramatic monologue unified by its voice but broken up into very short, fashionably Imagist sections. The poem is about a ferry trip Williams took home to New Jersey after apparently staying up all night on duty in a New York City hospital. The fifteen short sections of the poem, composed of things he saw and imagined on his way home, tend to separate into independent details and different moods, thus pulling against the centripedal forces that a monologue should maintain. The shortness of the stanzas and the incompleteness of the sentences intensify this fragmenting effect; the most common transition from one sentence fragment to the next is simply a dash and an "and":

---

① *Imaginations*,ed. Webster Scott (New York: 1970),23.

> – and the worn,
>
> blue car rails (like the sky!)
>
> gleaming among the cobbles! (*CP I* 101)

In addition, Williams uses the first person in only four out of seventeen sections and gives us few clues as to who is speaking and what action is taking place. All these aspects of the poem begin to displace the first-person speaker from the centre of this monologue, unlike what happens in a classic monologue by Robert Browning or even any of those in *Al Que Quere!*

This displacement may have been one reason why Williams subtitled the poem "Suite". The name primarily refers to the collection of impressions that make up the poem but may perhaps also be taken to refer to the "suite" of tones in his voice. There is first the sober, reflective voice of the opening section, in which Williams stands the genre of the exotic travel narrative on its head by focusing on the local and the familiar. "I have discovered," the poet reports portentiously, that

> the domes of the Church of
>
> the Paulist Fathers in Weehawken
>
> against a smoky dawn – the heart stirred –
>
> are beautiful as Saint Peters
>
> approached after years of anticipation. (*CP I* 100)

Then there is the exclamatory voice that takes over the poem after the *I* disappears in Section Ⅱ; it seems to be the voice not of a veteran traveler but of one experiencing the trip for the first time. It excitedly announces the details described in Section Ⅱ through Ⅶ with merely a dash and an *and* for each:

> – and from basement entries
>
> neatly coiffed, middle aged gentlemen
>
> with orderly moustaches and
>
> well-brushed coats (*CP I* 101)

In the middle of Section VIII, the poem modulates again, as Williams leaves the city behind to board the ferry. Being on the open water increases his excitement, and instead of merely naming objects exuberantly, as he did before, in section VIII and IX he addresses them directly and uses extravagant figures of speech as if to portray the excitement of being on the open water. The ferry, christened the Arden, is changed by Williams into a dream ship piloted by Shakespeare's Touchstone, while the river's brown waves become adorned with "circlets of silver" and the sky is turned into a magical seagull

> His spirit is
>
> a white gull with delicate pink feet
>
> and a snowy breast for you to
>
> hold to your lips delicately! (*CP I* 102)

In section XI the more sober narrator of Section I turns, speaking as authoritatively as he did in Section I, and on the same topic, too:

> Who knows the Palisades as I do
>
> knows the river breaks east from them
>
> above the city – but they continue south
>
> – under the sky- (*CP I* 102-103)

The emphasis here is on the importance of repeated, familiar experience, not the exclamatory revelations of the earlier sections. In Section XII,

Chapter 6
Impressionist Narrative in Williams' Poetry

Williams' mood continues to calm; he describes the long yellow rushes on the approaching New Jersey shore as if they lay still, "in contemplation." The excitement of the city streets and the open water ebbs as the ferry ride is near its end.

Sections X Ⅲ and X Ⅳ deal with death, and for the first time Williams' voice is tired, caustic, ironic:

> Work hard all your young days
>
> and they'll find you too, some morning
>
> staring up under
>
> your chiffonier at its warped
>
> bass-wood bottom and your soul –
>
> out! (*CP I* 103-104)

This memory, perhaps recalling a corpse Williams attended that morning, appears without apparent reason – nothing that he sees in the landscape would seem to remind him of death. It may be that Williams' slowly fading exuberance prompts it. But the slightly somber mood of these lines contrasts markedly with the unrestrained joy of the earlier sections, or with the joy that returns in the codalike last section of the poem as Williams tells the story of his all-nighter to his mother:

> Well, you know how
>
> the young girls run giggling
>
> on Park Avenue after dark
>
> when they ought to be home in bed?
>
> Well,
>
> that's the way it is with me somehow. (*CP I* 103-104)

Cynic, giggling girl, young doctor, experienced old-time who like Henry Thoreau or Whiteman knows the joys of traveling close to home – all these characters seem to have bought passage with Williams on the ferry. The poems' strength is that it makes his monologue dramatic and varied. But Williams would only have to vary and to juxtapose these voices more assertively and he would begin moving away from the form of the dramatic monologue altogether.

This is just what happens in the middle of "Overture to a Dance of Locomotives." Williams began by writing a monologue in a single mood, but he ended the poem with suite of contending voices. The slow meditation with which "Overture" opens is not unlike Sections XII or X III in "January Morning." Here is the third stanza:

> Covertly the hands of a great clock
>
> go round and round! Were they to
>
> move quickly and at once the whole
>
> secret would be out and the shuffling
>
> of all ants be done forever. (*CP I* 146)

The crowds streaming through the darkened corridors of Penn Station suggest Hades. This impression is strengthened by references elsewhere to "descending stairways" and "earthcolored walls of bare limestone" (*CP I* 146). But if these details suggest a lugubrious and bitter portrait of life in an Unreal City like that in Eliot's *The West Land*, other details in the same stanzas contradict.[①] Williams' description of the light in the cavernous

---

① Compare *The Waste Land*, I , 60-68:
    Unreal City,
    Under the brown fog of a winter dawn,
    A crowd flowed over London Bridge, so many,
    I had not though death had undone so many.
    Sighs, short and infrequent, were exhaled.
    And each man fixed his eyes before his feet.
    Flowed up the hill and down King William Street.

main hallway of the station, for example, implies that it is womblike: the light is "soft" and "rocks / to and fro, under the domed ceiling" (*CP I* 146). Trains then steam into the poem, filling it with their own raw power and dissipating any impression of a wasteland. The marmoreal tetrameter stanzas of the poem's melancholic monologue are shattered by dashes, frequent stanza breaks, eruptive rhythms, and new voices:

> two – twofour – twoeight!
>
> Porters in red hats run on narrow platforms.
>
> This way ma'am!
>
> > – important not to take
>
> the wrong train!
>
> > – Lights from the concrete
>
> ceiling hang crooked but –
>
> > Poised horizontal
>
> on glittering parallels the dingy cylinders
>
> packed with a warm glow – inviting entry –
>
> pull against the hour. But brakes can
>
> hold a fixed posture till –
>
> > The whistle! (*CP I* 146)

Williams ends his poem by comparing the train's androgynous sexual energy to the industrial power that is rebuilding America. The train's passenger cars are phallic, cylinders "packed with a warm glow," but they also seem feminine, "inviting entry." And both the train and the modern technology that it represents are participating in an unending "dance" of movement as "rivers are tunneled," "trestles / cross oozy swampland," and "rails forever parallel / return on themselves infinitely." "Overture to a Dance of Locomotives" begins with a single point of view but then rapidly, even discordantly increases the number of perspectives through which it views its subject. The repetitive motions that seemed so lifeless to the poet at the start of the poem "inevitable postures infinitely / repeated" is one of his meaning, a dance in which trains, passengers, and the entire city seem to be moving in time, on time.

Williams' poem should not be read as if its depiction of trains belongs to the ironic Modernist tradition of Eliot's *The Waste Land.* Although when the poem opens Williams sees the crowd as a dehumanized mob, by the middle of the poem the scene is portrayed more sympathetically, especially when we overhear a porter helping a woman find her train. For Williams, other more celebratory views of the urban world were possible, ones that did not gain their powers by interpreting modern life cynically or ironically. Williams thus uses ventriloquist techniques in "Overture" to a much different end than Eliot was soon to do in *The Waste Land.* Whereas all the voices in Eliot's poem except those chanting religious phrases are viewed ironically, Williams' voices are all examples of the city's productive "dance" of energy. "Overture" and a later poem from *Spring and All,* "Rapid Transit," are the only American poems of the period that do not turn a subway or an underground train journey into a trip through hell. As for Williams' American mentors, they are, first, Whitman, whose poems "Crossing Brooklyn Ferry," "To a Locomotive in winter," "Song of the Broad-Axe," and "Passage to India" saw American technology as yet another example of her spiritual and technological progress. "Overture to a Dance of Locomotives" may not be a fully unified work of art, but it gains interest precisely because of that fact; if the dominant mode at the start of the poem is irony, by the end Williams uses the essentially optimistic urban aesthetic of Whitman to exorcise it.

In impressionist writing, man is no longer seen as essentially one as man in the tradition writing.

> The very goal of the impressionists is the multiplication of the self. "I" is someone else. He is many. All the narrators are to some degree multiple personalities with multiple faces, seen at different periods of their lives, in different situations, by gossip and hearsay. (Kronegger 65)

When the narrator is alone in himself, he ceases being a single person. When he becomes aware of the multiple selves of his being, he is either expanding beyond his limits or plunging into dissolution. In many instances the narrator, having lost their lucid consciousness and their will to change the situation, is overcome by the presence of objects. In impressionist writing, man has no self-image: he is caught in a world where subject and object have merged to become one and the same. Such merging is certainly evident in these above poems of Williams.

6.2　Williams' Fragmental Narrative

Jesse Matz, a famous Literary impressionist from Harvard University, once advocated: "It doesn't choose surfaces and fragments over depth and wholes, but makes surfaces show depths, make fragments suggest wholes, and devotes itself to the undoing of such distinctions." (Matz 25) According to literary impressionists, every element of the text is useful for contributing to the final purpose, the impressionistic writers don't merely juxtapose all the unrelated fragments together without any aim. In fact, for impressionist the fragmentation and the juxtaposition are never self-contradictory. The impressionist writers do not narrate in an order way, they do not tell the event from the beginning to the end in the traditional way, but choose the limited narrative. They merely choose some fragmental pieces and casually show some of the scenes or images. All these elements are perfectly connected by their juxtaposition. Actually, in impressionist works, many fragmented elements are often juxtaposed together in order to attain a higher level of emotional impression. In Williams' poems, the impressionistic composition makes his poetry more gipping. The juxtaposition of fragments which are logically unconnected enables the readers to get a quite strong impression about the theme of the poetry in a very short time.

Williams' poems have numerous impressionistic features. Their forms are marked by fragmentation and juxtaposition. Many of the sentences in these poems are grammatical fragments (often signaled by dashes), and these fragments tend to cluster in groups without a set left-hang margin and with plenty of white space around the lines. The poems often speak in many voices, but sometimes one voice comes to dominate, usually that of the character who figures centrally in the poem's narrative. Some revel in employing a verbal version of impressionist quotation, juxtaposing "real" but also highly artificial "found" language with words that are poet's own. When they do this their intent is, the same as the impressionists, to question boundaries that have been drawn between "reality" and "art." These poems delight in the power of artifice, the mind's rage to order.

After including "Overture to a Dance of Locomotives" in *Sour Grapes* (1921), Williams became intrigued with the possibilities posed by the fragmented ending of that poem. In his next volume, *Spring and All* (1923), he published several poems, including two that directly pick up where his 1917 train poem left off – "Rapid Transit" and "The Rose".

In "Rapid Transit," Williams' use of quotation is a good deal more complex than in "Overture." It is perhaps partly inspired by Matthew

Josephson's article in *Broom* in praise of American advertising, "The Great American Billboard," which appeared in the November, 1922, issue while Williams was working on *Spring and All*. Williams quotes the kind of information we may read in a newspaper's investigative article:

> Somebody dies every four minutes
> in New York State –
>
> To hell with you and your poetry –
> You will rot and be blown (*CP I* 231)

An excerpt from what sounds like a cliché-ridden promotional brochure describing the places one may visit on New York City's transit system:

> Acres and acres of green grass
> wonderful shade trees, rippling brooks
>
> Take the Pelham Bay Park Branch
> of the Lexington Ave. (East Side)
> Line and you are there in a few
> minutes (*CP I* 232)

A scrap of a pop tune one might hum while driving "Ho for the open country;" an argument between a writer and one of his offended readers:

> To hell with you and your poetry –
> You will rot and be blown
>
> through the next solar system
> with the rest of the gases – (*CP I* 231-232)

And the kind of tip one could read in the public-service announcements displayed on buses and subway cars or mailed to drivers:

    AXIOMS

        Don't get killed

        Careful Crossing Campaign
        Cross Crossings Cautiously (*CP I* 232)

Such language introduces the same paradoxes into Williams' composition that the impressionist painters did in theirs. "Real" objects or "nonliterary" and merely referential language are often more stilted and artificial than the controlled, self-conscious artifice of art. The poem's title is rightly chosen. As readers, we get on board the poem for a rapid, exhilarating shuttle back and forth between the different ways in which we use and misuse language every day.

Williams' another famous poem in *Spring and All*, "The Rose" stresses above everything else the artist's responsibility to engender a second man-made order that may rival nature's own. The work is full of playful conflations of the real and the artificial, especially as they are revealed by the word *edge*, one of the key words in the poem. *Edge* comes to mean the physical edge of the rose petals, the edge of the poetic line as it ends on the page, the boundary between the physical rose and the roses constructed by the artist in painting and poetry, and, finally, the interface between traditional and new uses of the rose in art. Williams can achieve these simultaneous meanings for the word partly because he employs fragmentary, ambiguous syntax, as in the following lines, where the series of adjectives in the second stanza refer both to an actual flower petal and to love, to an artist's own work paying homage to the rose in metal, majolica, and other media both traditional and contemporary.

As Maria Elisabeth Kronegger claimed in his *Literay Impressionism*:

> Two things seem to be most striking in impressionist creations: On the one hand, there is the impressionist painter, composer and writer who, in wishing to recover man's wholeness, attaches his own intuitive being to the created being, and who, paradoxically, proceeds in fragmentary impressions, reflections, and illusions of the moment. On the other hand, these impressions of a world in dissolution add up to an autonomous work of art. Detached from traditional values, all artistic impressionist creations become autonomous entities... (Kronegger 21)

Each of these constructed worlds in "The Rose" is also autonomous. Williams therefore describes these artificial worlds as artificial roses placed at the edge of Nature's rose, adjacent to it physically and equal to it in importance:

> It is at the edge of the
> petal that love waits
>
> Crisp, worked to defeat
> laboredness – fragile
> plucked, moist, half-raised
> cold, precise, touching (*CP I* 195)

Williams' description of this imaginary still life assumes that a real rose petal has been included in the work (an impossibility, of course, at least for long, but easily conjured up in literature.)

Later in "The Rose" Williams seems to reject his previous attempts to describe the rose in order to improvise two more. He doesn't finish one, but the second is a conceit that, carefully elaborated, ends the poem:

> The place between the petal's
> edge and the
> From the petal's edge a line starts
> that being of steel
> infinitely fine, infinitely
> rigid penetrates
> the Milky Way
> without contact – lifting
> from it – neither hanging
> nor pushing – (*CP I* 195-196)

These last three stanzas of the poem have all the trademarks of the limited narration in literary impressionism: juxtaposed sentence fragments, including the "scrap" at the start of the quotation; a mixture of the intimate and the monumental; and a heady faith that man's reason (represented here by the steel line) has the right to penetrate, abstract, and reconstruct nature. A rose by any other name would smell as sweet, but it is only through our names and our conventions for using roses that we can know the rose at all or give its scent meaning. Williams implies that all "nature" (not just a single rose) is fundamentally engendered by the mind.

After Williams had decided that he could include many different voices within some of his dramatic monologues, he then had to decide whether to open up the form all the way, as he does in "Rapid Transit," juxtaposing as many voices as possible without letting a single one dominate, or just partially, including many voices but keeping them subordinate to one. "The Rose" in fact represents a compromise. In it, we are given different descriptions of its subject – indeed, it is as if at several points the poem includes its cancelled drafts in the final composition – but the figure of the poet-narrator remains dominant. He stands at the center of his composition, improvising order and commenting upon its importance.

"The Cod Head" (1932) appears to be a sort of literary still life created from memories of a summer trip Williams took with his wife in 1931 to the seacoast provinces of Canada. "The Cod Head" at first appears to be all fragmentation and no order. Here is the first stanza:

> Miscellaneous weed
> strands, stems, debris –
> firmament
>
> to fishes – (*CP I* 357)

Later on the syntax becomes even more splintered, confused sky and sea and night and day; it is as if Williams' dashes and line breaks, like the relentless surf, were pulverizing all they encounter:

> oars whip
> ships churn to bubbles –
> at night wildly
>
> agitate phospores –
> cent midges – but by day
> flaccid
>
> moons in whose
> discs sometimes a red cross
> lives – four (*CP I* 357-358)

A later comment on the poem that Williams made is so lucid that, after one has read the above lines, it may seem that he is speaking of a different work. He even explains the meaning of the "red cross discs": "Cod was the only thing being caught at that place (Labrador) and (I) had seen many of the assistant fishermen cutting up the fish preparatory to laying the flesh out on prepared boards to be sundried. You might, in the same poem, have wondered about the 'red across.' But there is actually a plainly marked red across, just like the ordinary 'plus' mark in arithmetic, figured on the back of the large jelly-fish or stingeree (stingever), seen so commonly in the water of Labrador..., I saw hundreds of the heads thrown back into the sea."[1] Admittedly, the "red across" and the "flaccid moons" in the poem are probably unintelligible to a reader without Williams' gloss. But this is the only time when Williams' impressionist fragmentation in this poem has been perhaps too severe. A supple organizing principle soon emerges upon rereading, and it turns out that it is the same one that Williams had used to order other less aggressively fragmented poems: he follows the imagined movement of the eye as it takes in the scene.

In this case, Williams imagines the journey a visionary eye might take as it views the water's surface, descends "four fathom" to the ocean's floor, then rises again, all the while without its version being clouded. After repeatedly struggling to find the best way of organizing his poem, Williams decided to mark the stages of his imaginary journey by sounding the fathoms as the poem moved along:

> moons in whose
>
> discs sometimes a red cross
>
> lives – four

---

[1] Williams to Kenneth Burke, 1945, quoted in Emily Mitchell Wallace, *A Bibliography of William Carlos Williams* (Middletown, Conn, 1968), 34.

fathom – the bottom skids

a mottle of green

sands backward –

amorphous waver –

ing rocks – three fathom

the vitreous

body through which –

small scudding fish deep

down – and

now a lulling lift

and fall –

red stars – a severed cod –

head between two

green stones – lifting

falling (*CP I* 358)

After opening the poem with a description of the many ways in which the surface of the water might be agitated (oars, propellers, flotsam, jellyfish), Williams dives down four fathoms, then moves up again amid a school of skittish fish at "three fathom," then breaches, floats, and rests, contemplating the lulling (rather than "agitated") lift and fall of the waves. Williams calculated contrasts between surface and depth and agitation and calm are less discernible in the earlier versions of the poem, principally because he had not yet hit upon the strategy of calling out the fathoms. Despite the broken miscellany of detail, then, a subtle but convincing order has been achieved; Williams is right to call it a "fragment." Moreover, the time he took in cutting, arranging, and revising his sentence fragments is indicative of the central aesthetic impressionistic poems, as different as they may appear on the surface: care and craft, order and arrangement, are paramount.

"The Sea-Elephant" is also a poem that greatly varies its voices and employs clipped sentence fragments marked by dishes. The poem begins with a description of a circus audience at Barnum& Bailey's Circus in Madison Square Garden in New York City, watching an elephant seal perform. The poet assumes several guises: a sideshow hawker exhibiting an exotic natural phenomenon:

> Ladies and Gentlemen!
>
> the greatest
>
> sea-monster ever exhibited
>
> alive (*CP I* 341)

A Sensible woman offended by the spectacle of the crowd and the imprisoned seal:

> (In
>
> a practical voice) They
>
> ought
>
> to put it back where
>
> it came from. (*CP I* 342)

A translator for the animal who speaks an ur-language filled with vowel-sounds and is hungry to gulp down or describe the entire world ("Blouaugh! ... / ... / I / am love. I am / from the sea – "); and the poet himself, who occasionally interrupts this lively chorus as a narrator might, describing the scene and reacting to it. The poet is both tender and mocking:

the gigantic

sea-elephant! O wallow

of flesh where

are

there fish enough for

that

appetite stupidity

cannot lessen? (*CP I* 341)

Yet like the woman in the audience, he pities the monster, noting its "troubled eyes – torn / from the sea" (*CP I* 342). That pity also extends toward the people in the audience, and himself. If the beast in the sea is love with all its primordial creative power, the beast captured and put on display must be a metaphor for love in its fallen, mundane form. Going to the circus to ogle freaks, beasts, and high-wire contortionists from the safety of the stands, the people in the crowd, suddenly, are forced to see themselves in the acts they watch. Each person sees that his own unnatural posturing in work and marriage is a show just as grotesque and comic as the one he comes to gawk at. The elephant seal thus admonishes the crowd, reversing who is in the ring and in the stands:

Blouaugh!

Swing – ride

walk

on wires – toss balls

stoop and

contort yourselves –

But I

am love. I am

from the sea – *(CP I* 342-343)[1]

As well as being an image of love, the huge, omnivorous sea beast also reminds Williams of the unlimited bounty, "a kind of heaven," that is spring. His description of the monster echoes several earlier passages in his poetry, especially the description of the coral island rising out of the sea in the poem dated "9 / 30" in *The Descent of Winter* (1927) and his many depictions of spring's birth in *Spring and All*. And it foreshadows several details in Williams' best elegy, "To Ford Madox Ford in Heaven" (1940). Williams first compares the sea elephant to spring as he watches it feed. With no more warning than a stanza break, he suddenly veers from his description of the beast feeding to these lines:

Sick

of April's smallness

the little

leaves – *(CP I* 341)

He then does not finish the thought but returns to the beast itself, mimicking its great throaty voice. At the poem's end, though, the analogy between spring and the seal surfaces again, in the form of two metaphors and a literary allusion.

---

[1] Williams also alludes, perhaps too elliptically, to the folklore traditionally associated with the beast, the stories about how sailors once saw a sea cow from a distance and thought they had sighted a mermaid. These legends are all the more ludicrous now that the cow can be seen closeup: "Strange head / told by sailors / rising / bearded to the surface." For another poem in which Williams compares love (and trees) to a beast "fresh-risen" from the sea, see "rain" (1929).

Williams compares the seal's breaching the ocean surface to the birth of an island and the arrival of spring; the entire wealth of the ocean, even the world, seems to gush forth from the beast's head and glisten in the sun. It is a kind of aquatic Genesis:

> the sea
>
> held playfully – comes
>
> to the surface
>
> the water
>
> boiling
>
> about the head the cows
>
> scattering
>
> fish dripping from
>
> the bounty
>
> of ... and Spring
>
> they say
>
> Spring is icummen in – (*CP I* 343)

Williams retains the essential features of sublime ode, such as its effusive style, contrasting voices, and elevated subject matter in this poem. It is essentially a short song in praise of spring. The lyric using sentence fragments and polyphony to celebrate creation and order may most appropriately be called Williams' impressionist ode.

Chapter 7

Conclusion

In writing this book the author has had two main concerns. The first is to discuss, where possible, Williams' contact with impressionist painters and theories; the second is to apply this background material to a careful study of the poems themselves. Williams' close ties to the world of painting are apparent in many of his poems. Williams himself acknowledges the visual elements in his verse when he talks with Edith Heal, the editor of *I Want to Write a Poem.* He tells about revising the poem, "The Nightingales, " (1921) in order "to make it go faster…" and says with apparent pleasure, "See how much better it conforms to the page, how much better it looks?" (Heal 66) In his autobiography, Williams also suggests that "poetic form is never more than an extension of content." (*Au* 330)

Williams himself seems to avoid making subjective comments on the concrete visual techniques in the creation of a visual poetry. In fact, Williams' use of techniques associated with different schools of painting. From the actual content of his poetry, the present research demonstrates that the impressionist technique relies heavily on his poems. In this study, the interplay between the observer and the observed, the act of perception, special time, and impressionist narrative, as the most important characteristics of literary impressionism, are all dealt with in the early poetry of William Carlos Williams.

Chapter 7
Conclusion

Characterized as a spirit of innovation, impressionism provides young Williams a brand new act of seeing. From the book we can find that Williams' ideas about verse writing and Williams' sense of things follow the way of impressionism. By insisting on "no ideas but in things" Williams has forced his readers (many of them poets themselves) to discard their assumptions about the world, assumptions, for the most part, that permit men to avoid having to look at things; he has forced them to exam the objects in his poems for what they are in themselves, not for what they represent. The impressionist theory also explains why Williams' reader sometimes feels that he is seeing the poem: such graphic depictions bring the reader much closer to a simultaneous experiencing of the whole poem, perhaps because he unconsciously realized the appropriateness of a poem's punctuation and line length. Certainly, the impressionist painting may be highly imaginative in his presentation of light and color, atmospheric conditions, or inanimate objects, but his observer knows he is looking at something that must exist in the tangible world. When the reader finishes a poem in which Williams presents his material as an impressionist painting world, when he looks at that poem printed on the page as an entity in his own right rather than as a collection of worlds, he begins to realize that the poem exists between two worlds, one verbal, the other visual. Because this kind of poem becomes its subject matter as completely as is verbally possible, the poem begins to have a tangible reality which the reader senses. In its imitation of an impressionist painting, the poem also acquires a reality akin to that which a painting always possesses; like a painting, it depicts a tangible object, and it gains independent existence through the process of depiction. The poem's inclusion of painting devices eventually forces the reader to look at the form of the entire poem as a whole, just as an observer frequently responds to a painting in its totality.

Demonstrating these impressionistic features in Williams' early poetry and exploring the sources of his visual art background can more fully explain the complexity of Williams' poetics, understand the significance of Williams' verse, and of course help Williams' reader understand his poetry more deeply. William Carlos Williams is able to create a surrealistic world in his poetry; he is also capable of producing an impressionistic poem in which light and color interplay as they often do in the paintings of the impressionist painters. Taught meticulously and durably by the painters whose works Williams loved, Williams may not always have understood what he saw, but in his bright joy for the shape of things, and in his fiery determination to lift the small beauties of our everyday environment to the center of our vision, he has indeed given the world a most valuable legacy: the gift of accurate observation. In the best of his early poems he has, like Cézanne, Monet, or Demuth, the master painters he most admired, secreted his meaning: the shrewd and durable sight of his extraordinary eye.

William's later work also reveals the obvious influence from impressionism. Two of Williams' later poems, "Perfecton" (1944) and "Choral: the Pink Church" (1949), are deliberately put in this book to prove that impressionistic techniques are not only applied in his early poems but also involved in his later ones. In this way, the book attempts to set examples to show that impressionism actually becomes an universal character of all his works. After impressionism, Williams' interest in the ideas and achievements of the visual arts continue to grow, and some of these interests are new, he begins to feel that cubism and Dadaism are important. The paintings and theories of these new arts excite him, and he makes friends with many new painters, continues to follow the works of them. He continues to look to the visual arts as a source and parallel for his work for the rest of his life. Williams' essays such as "An Afternoon with Tchelitchew" (1937, *ARI*, 119-123), "Walker Evans: American Photographs" (1938, *ARI*, 136-139), "E. E. Cummings's Paintings and Poems" (1954, *ARI*, 233-237), and "Brancusi" (1955, *ARI*, 246-254) also document his continuing interest in the modernist visual arts. It is found throughout the novels and poetry, from "Dev" Evans of *A Voyage to Pagany* (1928) exploring his responses to the achievements of France and Italy, to the late poem "Tribute to the Painters" which celebrates

> the knowledge of
>
> the tyranny of the image
>
> and how
>
> man
>
> in their designs
>
> have learned
>
> to shatter it (*PB* 135-137)

and to the "Pictures from Breughel" sequence.

The direction of Williams' later work is towards a reconciliation with art of the past that allows this art to speak through the poet far more on its own terms than his earlier poetry would allow. The pressures of the past in the earlier work are shaped to a design that stresses the exigencies of the present, the urgent need for contemporary expression. In the later work, the past comes more to achieve an equal status with the present in the shaping of the poem, a resolution often marked by a return of that reflective quality that Williams has exercised from his early poetry, such as *Kora in Hell* and *Spring and All*. Fine as much as this later verse is, it often lacks the dynamics of the conflicting, overlapping, internally generated patterns that charge his early poetry and give shape to its self-made, self-referential history. Nevertheless, the relationship of Williams' visual arts interests to this later work is an important subject in itself, and has been the focus of two discussions, Henry M, Sayre's, *The Visual Text of William Carlos Williams* (1983) and Dickran Tashjian's *William Carlos Williams and the American Scene, 1920-1940* (1978). Those interested in this study refer to these texts.

Bibliography

[1] ALTIERI CHARLES. Painterly abstraction in modernist American poetry: The contemporaneity of modernism [M]. Cambridge: Cambridge University Press, 1989.

[2] ALTIERI CHARLES. The art of twentieth-century American poetry: modernism and after [M]. Malden: Blackwell Publishing Ltd., 2006.

[3] ALTIERI CHARLES.Self and sensibility in contemporary American poetry [M]. Cambridge: Cambridge University Press, 1984.

[4] ALTIERI CHARLES. Act & Quality: a theory of literary meaning and humanistic understanding [M]. Amherst: The University of Massachusetts Press, 1981.

[5] AXELROD STEVEN GOULD. Critical essays on William Carlos Williams [M]. New York: G. K. Hall & Co. Macmillan Publishing Company, 866 Third Avenue, 1995.

[6] BECK JOHN. Writing the radical center: William Carlos Williams, John Dewey, and American cultural politics [M]. Albany: State University of New York Press, 2001.

[7] BENDER TODD K. Literary impressionism in Jean Rhys, Ford Madox Ford, Joseph Conrad, and Charlotte Bronte [M]. New York and London: Garland, Ink., 1997.

[8] BREMEN BRIAN A. William Carlos Williams and the diagnostics of culture[M]. New York: Oxford University Press, 1993.

[9] BRESLIN JAMES E. William Carlos Williams: an American artist [M]. New York: Oxford University Press, 1970.

[10] BURKE KENNETH. William Carlos Williams: two judgements [M]//William Carlos Williams: a collection of critical essays. J HILLIS MILLER, ENGLEWOOD CLIFFS, ed. New Jersey: Prentice Hall, 1966: 47-61.

[11] CALLAN RON. William Carlos Williams and transcendentalism: fitting the crab in a box [M]. New York: St. Martin's Press, 1992.

[12] CAPPUCCI PAUL R. William Carlos Williams, Frank O'Hara, and the New York Art Scene [M]. Madson and Teaneck: Fairleigh Dickinson University Press, 2010.

[13] CHENEY SHELDON. A primer of modern art [M]. New York: Liverlight, 1966.

[14] CONRAD BRYCE. Refiguring America: a study of William Carlos Williams' In the American Grain [M]. Urbana and Chicago: University of Illinois Press, 1990.

[15] CRAWFORD T HUGH. Modernism, Medicine, & William Carlos Williams [M]. Norman and London: University of Oklahoma Press, 1993.

[16] DIGGORY TERRECE. William Carlos Williams and the ethics of painting [M]. Princeton: Princeton University Press, 1991.

[17] DIJKSTRA BRAM. The hieroglyphics of a new speech: Cubism, Stieglitz, and the early poetry of William Carlos Williams [M]. Princeton: Princeton University Press, 1969.

[18] DIJKSTRA BRAM. A recognizable image: William Carlos Williams on art and artists. New York, New Directions, 1978.

[19] DOYLE CHARLES. William Carlos Williams and the American poem [M]. London: Macmillan Press. Ltd., 1982.

[20] DOYLE CHARLES. William Carlos Williams: the critical heritage [M]. London, Boston and Henley: Routledge & Kegan Paul Ltd., 1980.

[21] ELIOT T S. Selected essays[M]. New York: Harcourt, Brace & Co., 1932.

[22] ELLIOT EMORY, et al. Columbia literary history of the United States [M]. New York: Columbia University Press, 1988.

[23] ENGELS JOHN. The Merrill Guide to William Carlos Williams [M]. Columbus, Ohio: Charles E. Merrill Publishing Company, 1969.

[24] FARNHAM EMILY. Charles Demuth: behind a laughing mask [M]. Norman: University of Oklahoma Press, 1971.

[25] FISHER WIRTH, ANN W. William Carlos Williams and autobiography: the woods of his own nature [M]. University Park and London: The Pennsylvania State University Press, 1989.

[26] FORD MADOX FORD. Critical writing of Ford Madox Ford [M]. USA: University of Nebraska Press, 1964.

[27] FRAIL DAVID. The early politics and poetics of William Carlos Williams[M]. London: UMI Research Press, 1987.

[28] GELPI ALBERT. A coherent Splendor: the American poetic renaissance (1910-1950) [M]. Cambridge: Cambridge University Press, 1987.

[29] GOTTESMAN RONALD, et al. The Norton anthology of American Literature [M]. Vol 2. New York: W. W. Norton & Company, Inc., 1979.

[30] GUNSTEREN, JULIA VAN. Katherine Mansfield and literary impressionism [M]. The Netherlands: Amsterdam- Atlanda, GA. 1990.

[31] HALTER PETER. The revolution in the visual arts and the poetry of William Carlos Williams [M]. Cambridge: Cambridge University Press, 1994.

[32] HAUSER ARNOLD. The social history of art [M]. STANLEY GODMAN, trans. New York: Random House, 1951.

[33] HEAL EDITH. I wanted to write a poem: the autobiography of the works of a poet [M]. New York: New Directions, 1978.

[34] HIGH PETER B. An outline of American literature [M]. London Longman Group UK Limited, 1986.

[35] KENNER HUGH. The Pound Era. 1971[M]. London: Pimlico, 1991.

[36] KONNEGGER, MARIA ELIZABETH. Literary impressionism [M]. New Haven, conn: College & University Press, 1973.

[37] LODGE DAVID. 20th century literary criticism [M]. London and New York: Longman, 1983.

[38] LUBBOCK PERCY. The craft of fiction [M]. New York: Viking Press, 1957.

[39] LUCEI-SMITH EDWARD. Visual arts in the twentieth century [M]. London: Laurence King, 1996.

[40] LYNTON NORBERT. The story of modern art [M]. London: Phaidon Press Limited, 1992.

[41] MACGOWAN CHRISTOPHER J. William Carlos Williams' early poetry: the visual arts background [M]. Ann Arbor: UMI Research Press, 1984.

[42] MACLEOD GLEN. The Cambridge companion to modernism [M]. Shanghai Foreign Language Education Press, 2000.

[43] MARLING WILLIAM. William Carlos Williams and the painters, 1909-1923 [M]. Athens: Ohio University Press, 1982.

[44] MARIANI PAUL. William Carlos Williams: a new world naked [M]. New York, London: W. W. Norton & Company, 1981.

[45] MARKOS DONALD W. Ideas in things: the poems of William Carlos Williams. London and Toronto: Associated University Presses, 1933.

[46] MARLING WILLIAM. William Carlos Williams and the Painters, 1909-1923 [M]. Athens, Ohio: Ohio University Press, 1982.

[47] MARZAN JULIO. The Spanish American roots of William Carlos Williams [M]. Austin: University of Texas Press, 1994.

[48] MATZ JESSE. Literary impressionism and modernist aesthetics [M]. Cambridge: Cambridge University Press, 2001.

[49] MILLER HILLIS. Poets of reality: six twentieth century writers [M]. Cambridge: Harvard University Press, 1965.

[50] MORRIS DANIEL. The writing of William Carlos Williams: publicity for the self [M]. Columbia and London: University of Missouri Press.

[51] NAGEL JAMES. Stephen Crane and literature impressionism [M]. University Park and London: The Pennsylvania State University Press, 1980.

[52] OLIPHANT DAVE, et al. WCW & Others: essays on William Carlos Williams and his association with Ezra Pound, Hilda Doolittle, Marcel Duchamp, Marianne Moore, Emanuel Romano, Wallace Stevens, and Louis Zukofsky [M]. Austin: The Harry Ransom Humanities Research Center, the University of Texas at Austin, 1985.

[53] ORTEGA Y GASSET. "The dehumanization of art" and other writings on art and Culture [M]. New York: Doubleday, 1956.

[54] OSTROM ALAN. The poetic world of William Carlos Williams [M]. London and Amsterdam: Carbondale and Edwardsville Southern Illinois University Press, 1966.

[55] PERHINS DAVID. A history of modern poetry: modernism and after[M]. Cambridge: Bellnap Press of Harvard University Press, 1996.

[56] PETERS JOHN G. Conrad and impressionism [M]. Cambridge: Cambridge University Press, 2001.

[57] Qian Zhaoming. Orientalism and modernsm: the legacy of China in Pound and Williams [M]. London: Duke University Press, 1995.

[58] RAPP CARL. William Carlos Williams and romantic idealism [M]. Hanover and London: University Press of New England, 1984.

[59] REWALD JOHN. The history of impressionism [M]. New York: The Museum of Modern Art, 1961.

[60] REXROTH KENNETH. American poetry in the twentieth century [M]. New York: The Seabury Press, 1973.

[61] RIDDEL JOSEPH N. The inverted bell: modernism and the counterpoetics of William Carlos Williams [M]. Clinton, Massachusetts: The Colonial Press Inc., 1974.

[62] ROSENFELD PAUL. By way of art: criticisms of music, literature, painting, sculpture, and the dance [M]. New York: Coward-McCann, Inc., 1928.

[63] SAYRE HENRY M. The visual text of William Carlos Williams [M]. Urbana and Chicago: University of Illinois Press.

[64] SCHMIDT PETER. William Carlos Williams, the arts, and literary tradition [M]. Baton Rouge and London: Louisiana State University press, 1988.

[65] SIRAGANIAN LISA. Modernism's other work: the art object's political life [M]. New York: Oxford University Press, 2012.

[66] SMITH PAUL. Impressionism beneath the surface [M]. New York: Harry N. Abrams, Incorporated, 1995.

[67] STOWELL H PETER. Literary impressionism, James and Chekhov [M]. Athens: The University of Georgia Press, 1980.

[68] TAPSCOTT STEPHEN. American beauty: William Carlos Williams and the modernist Whitman [M]. New York: Columbia University Press, 1984.

[69] TASHJIAN DICKRAN. William Carlos Williams and the American scene, 1920-1940[M]. Berkeley, Los Angeles, London: The University of California Press.

[70] TATE ALLEN. Collected essays [M]. Denver: Alan Swallow, 1959.

[71] THIRLWALL JOHN C. The selected letters of William Carlos Williams [M]. New York: McDowell, Obolensky Inc., 1957.

[72] TOMLINSON CHARLES. William Carlos Williams: a critical anthology [M]. Harmondsworth: Penguin, 1972.

[73] TOWNLEY ROD. The early poetry of William Carlos Williams [M]. Ithaca and London: Cornell Press, 1975.

[74] WAGNER LINDA WELSHIMER. Interviews with William Carlos Williams: "speaking straight ahead" [M]. New York: New Directions Publishing Corporation, 1976.

[75] WALLACE EMILY MITCHELL. A bibliography of William Carlos Williams [M].Middletown, Conn: Wesleyan University Press, 1968.

[76] WEAVER MIKE. William Carlos Williams: the American background [M]. Cambridge: Cambridge University Press, 1971.

[77] WHITAKER THOMAS R. William Carlos Williams [M]. Boston: Twayne Publishers, A Division of G.K. Hall & Co., 1989.

[78] WILLIAM CARLOS WILLIAMS. The autobiography of William Carlos Williams [M]. New York: New Directions Publishing Corporation, 1967.

[79] WILLIAM CARLOS WILLIAMS. Selected essays of William Carlos Williams [M]. New York: New Directions Publishing Corporation, 1969.

[80] WILLIAM CARLOS WILLIAMS. The collected poems of William Carlos Williams [M]. LITZ, WALTON, CHRISTOPHER MACGOWAN, Ed. 2 vols. Rev. ed. New York: New Directions Publishing Corporation, 1984.

[81] WILLIAM CARLOS WILLIAMS. Imaginations [M]. WEBER SCHOTT, ed. New York: New Directions Publishing Corporation, 1933.

[82] WILLIAM CARLOS WILLIAMS. Yes, Mrs. Williams: a personal record of my mother [M]. New York: McDowell, Obolensky Inc., 1959.

[83] WILSON JOHN J. William Carlos Williams & Harold Norse: the American idiom [M]. San Francisco: Bright Tyger Press, 1990.

[84] WITEMEYER HUGH. Pound/Williams: selected letters of Ezra Pound and William Carlos Williams [M]. New York: New Directions Publishing Corporation, 1996.

[85] ZINNES HARRIET. Ezra Pound and visual arts [M]. New York: New Directions Publishing Corporation, 80 Eighth Avenue, 1980.

[86] 陈建国. 诗歌·自我·人生——弗罗斯特和威廉姆斯之比较研究[J]. 外国文学, 1997(2):3–5.

[87] 丰子恺. 西洋艺术史[M]. 上海：上海古籍出版社，1999.

[88] 丰子恺. 绘画与文学·绘画概况[M]. 长沙：湖南文艺出版社，2001.

[89] 耿幼壮. 威廉斯与中国诗[J].博览群书, 2002(2): 66-70.

[90] 河清. 现代与后现代[M]. 杭州：中国美术学院出版社，1998.

[91] 李广元.《色彩艺术学》。哈尔滨：黑龙江美术出版社，2000.

[92] 李小洁. 论威廉·卡洛斯·威廉斯诗歌的色彩艺术[J]. 江汉论坛, 2003(2):3-5.

[93] 李小洁. 论威廉·卡洛斯·威廉斯的空间化诗歌[J]. 外国语言文学, 2009(3): 147-154.

[94] 李增. 威廉·卡洛斯·威廉斯诗歌新论[J]. 东北师范大学学报（哲学社会科学版）,1999(5), 14-77.

[95] 瓦尔特赫斯. 欧洲现代画派画论[M]. 宗白华，译. 桂林:广西师范大学出版社，2002.

[96] 吴甲丰. 印象派的再认识[M]. 北京：三联书店，1980.

[97] 杨霭琪. 谈印象派绘画[M]. 北京：人民美术出版社，1979.

[98] 张强. 意象派、庞德和美国现代主义诗歌的发轫[J]. 外国文学研究, 2001(10): 38-44.

[99] 张跃军. 美国性情——威廉·卡洛斯·威廉斯的实用主义诗学[M]. 合肥：安徽文艺出版社，2006.

Appendix

Illustrations

Figure 1   *Impression, Sunset* **(1873) by Claude Monet**

Figure 2   *The Umbrella* **(1881-1885)by Auguste Renoir**

Figure 3   Renoir's *Moulin de la Galette* (1876) by Auguste Renoir

Figure 4   *Les Courses de Chevaux* (1885-1888) by **Edgar Degas**

Figure 5   *Terrace at Sainte-Adresse* **(1867) by Claude Monet**

Figure 6   La Cathedrale de Rouen – plein soleil (1894) by Claude Monet

Figure 7 *Femme a l'Ombrelle* **(1886) by Claude Monet**

Figure 8 *L'Eglise d'Auvers* **(1890) by Van Gogh**

Figure 9 *On the Seine at Bennecourt* **(1868) by Claude Monet**

Figure 10 *Bathers at La Grenouillere* **(1869) Claude Monet**

Figure 11   *Norwegian landscape in Winter* (1895) by Claude Monet

Figure 12   *Sunflowers* (1881) by Claude Monet

Figure 13 *I Saw the Figure 5 in Gold* **(1928) by Charles Demuth**